The Art of Falling in Love with Your Fake Fiancé

ANNE KEMP

For the people out there who struggled as kids to figure out where they fit in, only to find their people once they took a chance on themselves. Maybe it was through theatre or art, or spending afternoons at the school library. Maybe you were at home reading, lost in the pages knowing you could escape between the covers because it was safe there.

I get it. I see you.
Anne x

Content Warnings

Like all of my books, this one IS a lighthearted and fun romantic comedy, but there are subjects mentioned in this book such as:

*parents passing away (in the past)
*foster family upbringing
*guardianship/custody case over a ten-year-old

ONE

Georgie

"Ready for your Fifteen Minutes?" I call out as the room of people facing me cheers. Handing the microphone over to tonight's volunteer host, I'm fighting my lips so they don't show my gums. My smile is that wide.

I could never have expected my little Pages and Prose Bookshop stuffed full of people like it is tonight. Ever. When I got the idea a few months back to start hosting open mics here once a week, I wanted to try something different. A "creative speakeasy" if you will. See if any residents of Sweetkiss Creek were hiding away in their homes and not showing off their talents.

Boy, did I find my people. Beatnik poets, solo guitar acts, interpretive dancers (looking at you and your seventy-five-year-old badass self, Mrs. Linden), and even stand-up comics.

A familiar face appears in front of me. He's got to be in his teens, maybe a senior at the local high school. It's hard to tell his age, but he spends at least two afternoons a week here after class perusing the shelves.

"Hey, Miss Simpson, do you have enough power in this place that I could bring my band next week?"

"Please, call me Georgie," I say. Even though I'm cringing inwardly, I work hard to not show how my insides feel on the outside. "But, no. Unfortunately, we won't be able to do full bands, but maybe one day?" I hold up crossed fingers as I walk away. I love supporting the local arts, but someone's first garage band in this small store would be pushing my luck. And all of our eardrums.

I make my way through the throng back to my perch on the other side of the counter. I guess since I'm the owner of the store it's my reserved spot. I keep the sign-in list up there for folks who want a go at the mic for fifteen minutes. That's why tonight is called 'Fifteen Minutes of Fame', so anybody can have a chance. Anybody within reason, but yes, anybody.

There's a temporary stage that my friends helped me build. Don't worry, it's sturdy. I tested it by having two of my biggest friends, Levi and his brother, Austin, jump up and down on it to make sure it wouldn't break. They both play in the NFL, so I figure if it can stand up to them and their muscly-body weight, it'll hold up for everyone else.

Looking around the room, I see the faces of so many of my new friends. Moving to Sweetkiss Creek a couple of years ago, I wasn't sure what I was in for. I just needed to start over. Fresh. Reinvent myself. I was living in New York City and had to get out. I hadn't known where I was going, I only knew I had to go.

It was very strategic how I chose to move here, too: I pulled out a map, closed my eyes, and placed my finger down on the paper. Sweetkiss Creek won.

My host for the night is local cop, and one of my best friends' husbands, Zac Wright. He waves to me as he heads around the counter, making a beeline for me. "Hey, Georgie," he says.

On stage, Mr. Johnson, the local florist whose business is only a few doors down from mine, starts his set. Who would have thought that a man so serious about roses is funny? Not me. Yet his sets here seem to be some of the most popular, and it makes me happy. His wife passed away last year, so to see him coming out of his shell like this makes me really happy. When I hear a loud "Woo hoo!" as he starts talking, I know his daughter is also in the audience giving him energy as he's up there, and it's gold.

"Great night tonight, Zac. Thanks for being my host with the most." I hold my hand up to high-five him. "Where's your wife? I thought she was coming."

"Etta had to drive Dylan and Reid to the airport. They're off to do their yearly EMT training. I think they're in Florida for a few weeks?" He shrugs as he leans against the counter. "All I know is we've got their dog."

Dylan is another one of my friends, and Reid is her husband. The dog in question is Max, and he likes to hang out with my dog. You know. When we go to the dog park. It's a whole vibe. IYKYK.

Honestly, I landed in the village of couple goals when I came here. I've never been so accepted by the popular girls, probably because I'm the one who lets her freak flag fly. It usually means I roll solo. I'm also so jealous, in the best way possible, of the relationshipping that happens here. I can only hope that I find someone here who's meant for me like my friends seem to have done.

Maybe one day.

"I'll text her this week and see if she wants to go to the dog park. Sounds like having Max along with your two dogs she'll need to get everyone worn out."

"Who knew doggy play dates were a whole thing?" Zac chuckles. "Love it." He cranes his neck and looks around. "I don't see Levi here tonight. Is he coming?"

The tiny flutter that happens inside of me when I hear Levi Porter's name never ceases to amaze me. I hesitated at becoming his friend. I even tried to talk myself out of it, especially once I realized the way I was starting to feel about him. But he's become a sugar addiction I don't want to quit. The TV show I have to tune into every week. That gas I put in my car.

Let me back up and explain. Levi Porter is one of the aforementioned NFL brothers, and he also happens to be one of my closest friends. We met a little over a year ago through a mutual friend, Riley. In the way small towns work, of course, he and Riley grew up together and were super tight, besties practically, but when she met and fell in love with her now husband Jake, she made sure to leave Levi with another female bestie who could be by his side.

That's me. Although I did pretty much offer myself up for the role.

"He picked up his godson yesterday and moved him to the farm," I share, keeping my voice low so I don't annoy anyone in the crowd.

Zac lets out a giant breath of air. "Wow. To go from a single man to a dad in only a matter of months... Crazy. How's he coping?"

"I'd say he's doing the best he can. I mean, he hadn't seen his friend for a few years and didn't even know he'd been made a guardian until the call came from the emergency room that there had been an accident."

Even though it was almost a year ago, the memory of the moment and Levi's worry is burned into my memory. We were at Riley's wedding when his phone rang. He'd left immediately to go to the hospital in New York where his friends had been rushed after a horrible fire.

"Isn't there anyone else who can take the boy in?" Zac asks.

I shrug. I know that there is, and she's waiting in the wings like a crazed stand-in on opening night, but I also know it's a source of contention right now. "Maybe. We'll see."

Applause interrupts us, signaling the end of Mr. Johnson's set and also cueing Zac to bring another tribute to the stage. He takes the mic and easily addresses the room, no anxiety at all, just him chatting with the people. If I was up there, I'd have heart failure. I can get on stage long enough to introduce the evening and the host, but that's it. I love being excited; I'm just not a fan of being a central part of it, if you know what I mean.

Zac calls the next act up to the mic, a newbie here named Bex Madden who's holding her guitar in one hand as she settles in behind the mic to sing a few songs. She only started coming two weeks ago and I'm glad she did—she's a crowd-pleaser for sure. Her voice is smooth and angelic; someone compared her to a softer version of Adele, which I found interesting.

As Bex strums the first few chords, I look around, and after checking the time and a peek at who is left on the list, figure I can do some work to get ready for closing. Because of the noise ordinance, we can't be here after eleven at night, which is fine with me. I need to be home and asleep by eleven-thirty if I can help it. A lady needs eight hours of solid rest after a busy day like I've had.

Pages and Prose is small but mighty. The interior is lined with five rows of shelves, each overflowing with books of all genres, from classic literature to contemporary bestsellers. When I was shopping to outfit the store, I picked out shelves made of dark wood, giving the bookstore a rustic and timeless feel. Soft lighting, turned down low for the open mic night, usually casts a gentle glow over the rows of books, creating a cozy ambiance that invites readers to explore.

The stage area is surrounded by comfy seating, including plush armchairs and sofas, where customers can relax and enjoy the performances. About six months ago, I added a small cafe area, where you can sit and enjoy a cup of coffee or tea while flipping through the pages of a new book. The walls are adorned with artwork from local artists, adding to the charm and character of the space. I really wanted this to be a retreat for book lovers, but also a place for locals to come and feel creative.

I make my way down one of the rows, straightening shelves and reordering books that I find out of place. Bex sings about heartbreak, but it's so poetic that I get lost in the melody...as do the other patrons, evidenced by their singing along. She's only been here a few times and she's already getting groupies. I love that for her.

I quickly go down a second row, find some kids books stuffed into the YA section, and round the end cap to head to the back of the store and put them away. It's where I've set up a small children's area with a little table and chairs and a toy box. It's the perfect spot for worn-out moms to come and let their kids play while they shop. I even pull babysitting some days, so they can have a cup of coffee and a time-out.

It's when I get to the back of the store I notice a shadowy figure out of the corner of my eye. A slight figure, with a baseball hat pulled down low across their face and wearing an oversized sweatshirt, stands with their back to the room, shoulders hunched. Clapping fills the air around me as I freeze in place, staying close to the shelves so as not to disturb the stranger. My stomach flips in horror as I watch this person take a book off the shelf and, as they whip their head from left to right, lift their T-shirt and stuff it inside their pants, laying their shirt back down on top of it.

No. Way. A shoplifter? In my store? I feel the heat of indignation rising up inside of me as I walk over and, without even thinking, grab their wrist.

"Hey," the young man cries out in surprise. "What's that for?"

Grasping the bottom of his shirt, I tug it up, revealing the book held in place against the young man's body by the elastic of his pants.

"To find out why you're trying to borrow that."

As the applause around us dies down, I hear Zac's voice on the mic as he introduces the next act. Clyde Paulson and his puppets. That's going to be interesting with a splash of creepy.

The kid rolls his eyes. "I'm not borrowing it. Duh."

So I roll mine, too. "You obviously don't understand when someone is using sarcasm as a deflector." I pull the book from his pants and give the elastic of his super-tight sweats an extra tug, allowing it to snap back with a *thwack* against his skin.

"Ow." Dark eyes look into mine. "What was that for?"

"Gee, I just don't know," I say, shaking my head and tucking the book under my arm. I have never had to deal with this before. I don't know what I'm going to do with this kid, I just know I have to do something. The only thing I can think to do is to take the boy to the counter. I'm in shock. "Come with me."

In that split second, this rogue criminal makes a decision. Flicking his eyes toward the exit on the other side of the room, he looks back at me. Surely he's not considering running? With all of these people around? However, as I let my eyes sweep the room again, everyone is focused on Clyde as he takes to the small stage, even Zac. I start to call out for some help, but movement pulls my attention back to the kid. His eyes shift downward, then to mine once more. We're both seeing his way out at the same time, and my stomach flips anxiously. I hate this.

"Nah, lady. I'm out," he snarls as he takes off running, barreling toward the door.

No. Way.

To get to the door, he has to make his way through the crowd, which he does almost expertly. I'm on his heels, trying to at least reach out and grab him. I didn't even want to punish him, just ask why he needed to steal.

Now, it's about not letting him get away.

He's like a ballerina, moving with grace avoiding bodies as they stand up or chairs as they're scooted backwards. Me? I'm a bull in a China shop. Stopped and blocked each step. By the time I open my mouth to yell for help, he's pushed the door open, bringing in a big ole' blast of warm summer night air, and he's out on the sidewalk. No good. By the time I reach him, he'll have all of Sweetkiss Creek to use as his hiding spot.

I burst out the door behind him, not sure what I'll find when I get out there myself, and I hear someone behind me. A quick glance over my shoulder tells me Zac is on my heels.

On the side of the main street, I pause, catch my breath, and look around.

"What's going on?" Zac asks, halting beside me.

I open my mouth to answer, but someone nearby interrupts.

"What's wrong, guys?"

Spinning on my heel, I'm super surprised, and really low-key happy, to find Levi standing in front of me—and there's a certain rug rat tucked under his arm. Like he's delivering me a present.

My hero.

"Trying to catch up with him," I pant, pointing to the young boy standing with him. Now that we're out of the dark store and standing under a streetlight, I can see his face clearly. He's so young. If I had to guess, I'd say he's ten or eleven, but who am I to know? I can only count in terms of dog years, if we're honest. Let's just say my maternal clock has never really gone off, so it's one alarm that may be permanently on snooze.

"This guy?" Levi asks, a huge grin spreading across his face. "Have you guys already met?"

I'm struggling here. My eyes flick to Zac's, and thankfully, he looks as confused as I do.

"Met?" What is Levi saying?

"Georgie, Zac," Levi says, smiling from ear to ear as he steps back and claps the young man on his shoulder, "this is Duncan Livingston. My godson."

TWO

Levi

When you haven't seen someone you've been hanging out with for a while, you would think they'd be happy to see you. It's not like I've been gone playing football for most of the year, or that we won the Super Bowl this year (well, we did, but I digress), so I'm not expecting a parade or fireworks, but a little excitement or even a cheer could go a long way for a guy.

Georgie blinks at me. She points to Duncan, who stands beside me in his usual position: arms crossed with a slight glower on his face. I think it's mandatory for all ten-year-olds.

"This is your godson?" she asks, her tone oddly accusatory.

"Sure is." My gaze drifts back and forth between her and Zac, trying to read the situation. I don't know Zac well, but well enough to know he's a cop on the Sweetkiss Creek police force. "Got him settled in at the farm today, then came into town for dinner and a few things." Focusing on Georgie, I give her my best grin. "Duncan wanted to stop by your bookshop and grab something. Did he find what he needed?"

Georgie shakes her head and laughs incredulously before

she puts me squarely in her sights and sighs. "Oh, he grabbed what he needed alright."

Judging by the way Zac's face twists and the lack of emotion he's showing, I have this weird gut instinct that Duncan's done something. I don't know what, but it's something that is *not* good.

"Do you want to tell me what's going on?" I say to Duncan, turning him around to face me and keeping my hands on his shoulders as I do so.

Duncan's eyes are blank as he shakes his head and purses his lips together tightly.

Staying in place, I turn my head so my gaze lands on Georgie, who crosses her arms over her chest.

She's almost apologetic as she waves a hand in the air, but I know her well enough and can tell when she's angry. She has this crease that shows up in between her eyebrows. It's like the muscles in her forehead give her away so you always know what she's feeling. "I caught him trying to steal a book." She puts her hand on her hip and pushes a few stray strands of hair out of her face.

Man. Probably not a good time to think about this, but she looks amazing when she's mad. Georgie is what I imagine a bohemian goddess to look like, with flowing, sun-kissed hair and eyes that sparkle with mischief and a hint of rebellion. Normally, she's a vision of effortless beauty, easily charming everyone around her with her laid-back attitude and free-spirited nature.

But when she's mad? Those fiery eyes of hers turn into laser beams that I swear, hand on heart, could cut through steel, and her normally serene expression transforms into an intense scowl. It's like watching a majestic lioness suddenly realizing she's stepped on a thorn–fierce, yet oddly adorable in her frustration.

"You came after *me*," Duncan fires back, pulling me back

into the moment, rolling his eyes as he looks up at me. "She snapped my waistband."

"Let them talk," Zac interjects, nodding toward Georgie as he stares down Duncan. Again, I don't know him very well, but Zac has the BEST resting cop face. The RCF…it even makes me a little nervous.

"Is this true?" I say, looking at Duncan incredulously. "Stealing is not what we do. I don't see you kicking off your summer in a good way if you're stealing things from my friend's store."

This is also not the best way to start out my off-season downtime nor to get to know people who I care about. In the back of my mind, I want to tell on this kid to his parents. But then I remember—I'm the one in charge. I'm his guardian now. And he's not like a machine you buy at the store; he didn't come with a manual. I'm figuring it all out as we go along.

Georgie holds up a book and waves it in the air for me to see. "Exhibit A."

"A cookbook?" My eyes slam back into Duncan's. He tries to look past my shoulder, but I maneuver so I'm in his line of sight. "Look at me, please. You tried to steal a cookbook by Jamie Oliver?"

This is no way for anyone to make a good impression. I was a kid once, not so horribly long ago, and I can remember testing boundaries and doing things that made my mother crazy. Plus, I have an older brother, so he was always there either cheering me on or acting as a partner in crime. Mostly cheering me on and talking me into things, so I get it. Such is kid life.

Duncan lets his gaze rest on the book, staring at it. He shrugs a shoulder, stuffing his hands in the front pockets of his jeans. "I wanted it."

"Well, you should have bought it," Georgie says. Judging

by the look on Duncan's face, her words are not well-timed.

"If I could pay for it, I would have," he all but growls. "But I'm a kid and don't have any money."

Zac winces as he takes a step back, which Duncan notices. "What did you do that for?"

"Son," Zac says with a chuckle, "you're proving to be braver than I would have thought. You realize you are sassing a Sweetkiss woman?" He lets out a low whistle, shaking his head. "If I were you, I'd start running again. Now."

"Stop it. No one is running anywhere any time soon," Georgie says. She takes a breath and closes her eyes, a move I recognize from the moments when she's needed to gather herself. She pauses for a few seconds before allowing her eyes to flutter open, looking at Duncan with more empathy than was there before. "But he's right. You don't need to talk to me like that. I'm not mad, Duncan. I just want to know why you did it."

Heat hits my cheeks. Not the fun kind, but the "I am so embarrassed right now" kind. It's my first week being officially in charge—my third day, actually, into this new life—and already I feel like I'm failing. Maybe some of us are not meant to be parents.

I turn to face Georgie, putting a hand on Duncan's shoulder. I'm hoping it comforts him, but I also want to be able to grab him if he starts to run away. "It doesn't matter why he did it, he did it. I'm sorry this happened."

Natural instinct leads me to reach into my pocket and pull out my wallet. As soon as I do, both Zac and Georgie give me their opinions.

"No way, Levi," Zac says, Georgie shaking her head beside him. "Not trying to be a buzzkill, but sometimes it helps if you do something more as punishment."

"I'm not going to let you arrest him..." I begin, and Zac laughs.

"No, not that either. Unless"—he snaps his head toward Georgie—"the owner wants to press charges?"

Georgie, with her arms still threaded tight in front of her, lets her eyes rock to each of us individually for a moment as she processes things. After a heavy thirty seconds of silence, which feels more like five minutes, she shakes her head and lets her arms drop to her side.

"No. I won't press charges," she says, letting her gaze rest on Duncan. "This time. But if you do it again, at my store or anyone else's, I think someone should hold you accountable."

Duncan's shoulders visibly drop as he exhales. I think it's the first time I've seen him relax like this since I met him. I'm trying to decide if that's a good thing or a bad thing when I get an idea.

"Can I see that?" I hold out my hand to Georgie, pointing to the cookbook in her hand. She gives it to me, and I open the cover and flip through its pages. It's just a cookbook about five-ingredient meals. I'm not sure what the cause for all of this is, but it's something Duncan wants.

"Who did you get it for?" I ask.

"Mrs. Porter," he squeaks, the ten-year-old beginning to shine through.

Closing the book, I turn to Duncan. "You wanted to get this for my mother?"

Eyes downcast, he nods.

A small group of people walk by us, making their way down the street, singing songs as a group. Duncan eyes them, his face clouding over. When I turn to see why he's so dark and stormy, I find what appears to be a family: father, mother, and two children all laughing and cajoling, and glowing, literally, with love. Looking back at Duncan, I see sadness reflected in his eyes and suddenly understand his reaction.

"Did Mrs. Porter do something that made you want to get her this book?" Georgie asks. When my eyes meet hers, something in the way she looks at me tells me she's beginning to understand his defensive ways as well.

Duncan lifts a shoulder, letting it drop heavily as he sighs. "She gave me a picture of my mom and dad. Framed. And put it in my bedroom for me to have on my first night."

I get a punch in my gut while my heart warms, but the layer of guilt is thick. What a dichotomy of emotions. I should have thought of that. Of course my mom would think to do it, a small thing but something that made him a little more comfortable.

She's a mom. She knows what to do. She got the manual....although after raising two boys mostly on her own, she probably helped write it.

"That was really nice of her to do," Georgie says, her voice soft with understanding. "I'm pretty sure she doesn't expect a gift from you as a thank you."

"I dunno," he eeks out.

Georgie takes the book from my grasp and hands it to Duncan. "So you know, I do offer a friends and family discount. If you want to buy it, you're entitled to twenty-five percent off."

Duncan, who's kept his gaze on the sidewalk, allows the ends of his lips to begin a slow ascent upward. Now, that's the trajectory I'm talking about.

"Really?" he murmurs as he looks at Georgie.

"Yes," Georgie says. "And it's your lucky night because this particular book is going on the clearance table tomorrow. For fifty percent off. So, if you want to buy it tonight, I'm prepared to give you a good deal."

As Duncan's expectant eyes land on mine, I feel this pull. The want to say yes, because that is a good deal, but also I feel like we're making it too easy on him. I mean, the kid did just try to steal this book and then run away with it, so there's that.

It's been a wild ride to get Duncan here, into my care. It

was only last year when his parents died. I was still processing the loss of them when my lawyer called and told me that Tom, one of my best buddies growing up, and Katie had made me his official guardian the day I became his godfather.

The part that's embarrassing here is in my naivety around being a godfather. I didn't realize this would be the case. I thought my job was to send presents for his birthday and holidays, and to touch base every now and then. I was prepared to be his buddy when he grew up, maybe hang out with him sometimes, take him to a football game or two. But no.

Apparently, while I was right about the fun and games, I missed the important gist of it all: the fact that godparents are supposed to have a special role in a kid's life, in some cases offering all kinds of lifelong support. Godparents bring experience and mentorship, and they can assist with personal development too. We're role models and in some cases, we're needed to help guide a child's growth emotionally, spiritually, and practically.

The main thing I learned (when I looked it up) is that the role of godparent depends on the wants and needs of the parents and what they expect when they ask someone to step up and be one. In this case, Tom and Katie had left explicit instructions in their wills that if anything happened to them, Duncan was to reside with me––and only me.

Of course this news did not go down well with everyone left in his family. His maternal grandmother is okay with it, but she lives in Hawaii and isn't in the financial nor the physical position to take care of a young man, but his paternal grandmother is a whole other story. When we'd picked up the last of his things today, she made sure to let me know that they weren't going to let this go without a fight.

Because, that's what everyone wants when they're in mourning. To fight.

"I don't think Duncan should get off that easy," I hear

myself say, which surprises me and Duncan.

"What?" he chokes.

"I just think you should have to work for it. There are no free rides."

The mechanical sound of a bell chiming nearby reminds me that Zac's standing with us. He pulls out his phone and looks at the screen before turning to us. "I've got to go guys." He looks at Georgie. "Etta's on her way home. I think all of the acts have gone already. You good to wrap up if I go?"

"Go home and be with your wife," Georgie says, waving a hand in the air. "And thank you."

We say our goodbyes, Georgie and I turning our attention back to Duncan at the same time.

"I have an idea," Georgie offers. "I've got a shipment of books coming in for a book signing this week. I was going to ask one of my old employees to come in and pull some extra hours to help me get ready for it, but I could use a hand if Duncan's up to it."

I guess there isn't any harm in letting Duncan hang out with Georgie at Pages and Prose, if she's really okay with it. "Are you sure about that?"

"Positive." She smiles at Duncan. "You're on summer break, right?"

He nods.

"Good. I need you here at ten tomorrow morning for your first shift. Wear comfortable clothes and be prepared to work. Lifting, moving tables, you get my drift."

Duncan nods again, but narrows his eyes. "Will I get paid?"

"Duncan." This kid. Got to hand it to him; he's asking for what he wants, but man the timing. "You were busted stealing. I don't think you get to do contract negotiations."

"It's okay, Levi," Georgie says as she holds up a hand signaling me to stop. She keeps her attention solely focused on

Duncan. "Me and you, we'll discuss your payment and hire terms tomorrow. I don't want to have any more discussion about it right now because I have a store full of people in there who need me to be back inside. Tomorrow, be here at ten."

I could kiss her. I want to scream at Duncan, but Georgie has just saved the day...for now.

"What do you say, Duncan?" I ask, nudging him in the back.

"That I'll see her tomorrow at ten?" he asks with genuine sincerity.

"Thank you is a good place to start," I hint.

"Oh," he says. "Yes. Thank you."

"You're welcome." Georgie makes her way back to the store, stopping to give my shoulder a squeeze as she passes by. "It's good to see you."

The simple acknowledgement she gives me is enough to send a tiny thrill down my spine. There's a strange sensation in my chest, like a group of tiny, clumsy acrobats performing somersaults. Like someone is inside the theater of my heart and they've decided to do a stand-up comedy routine, complete with poorly timed punchlines and awkward pauses.

"Sorry it's under these circumstances," I manage, ignoring my body's reaction and my internal monologue. "I was going to stop in tonight to say hi and introduce you to this guy, but..."

Georgie giggles. "He managed to meet me all on his own. It's all good. And it's nice to have you back in town."

The warmth of her hand feels nice on my shoulder. Familiar. The heat of her touch spreads through me, starting from the center of my chest and radiating outwards. Like a constant buzz of excitement and nervousness, a feeling that both exhilarates and calms my system.

Since I've been back for my off-season, I've wanted nothing more than to see her. When I do, my whole day brightens. Georgie's smile is like a beacon, drawing me in and making everything else fade into the background. In the past year, I've found myself wanting to impress her, to make her laugh, to just be around her as much as possible...but it's so hard to do when I'm on the road for my job. And now, having Duncan, everything's changed. I have no idea what life is going to be like over the next few weeks, much less the rest of the year.

All of this has led to my own small internal crisis: questioning my longevity in the NFL. My agent has my contract on his desk for five more years and I've asked him to hold negotiations. Because I'm not sure I want to keep playing.

Do I stay, do I go? I'm a guardian now. There's someone else relying on me. How do I navigate these waters?

Plus, there's this incredible woman in front of me. She thinks we're friends, and all I want is more. I can give her that, but she deserves someone who is here on a consistent basis. When she's not around, I catch myself thinking about her, wondering what she's doing, if she's thinking about me, too. It's like this magnetic pull that I can't resist, this constant longing to talk to her, to be with her.

"Oh, and one more thing," Georgie calls out, interrupting my thoughts as she wraps her hand around the door handle. "I say ten, Duncan, but I mean nine fifty-five. Where I come from, on time is late. And five minutes early is on time. Remember that, and we'll get along just fine."

She catches my attention and winks. "See you later?"

I smile and give her a nod. "You bet."

She opens the door of Pages and Prose and disappears from our sight, my heart both full from seeing her and also deflated because she's gone.

I don't know if she feels the same way about me, but I can hope—and maybe this summer I'll come clean about my feelings for her.

THREE

Georgie

The sun is barely even awake when I crawl out of bed in the morning. My feet hit the cold hardwood floor, and as much as I want to hop back into bed, I keep going. I only need the next twenty minutes for myself.

Stretching my arms overhead, I cast a glance to where my Rottweiler, Toto, lies on his giant memory foam dog bed. That was one purchase I splurged on, because he's my baby, and it's his favorite spot in the house. I sit and wait, wondering if he'll show any signs of movement like he might be rising for the day, but no. My big baby boy is apparently sleeping in.

Turning, I shuffle out into the living room and grab my yoga mat from the corner where I'd flung it yesterday before running out the door. Flicking it open, I lay it down in front of my TV. I have a few yoga videos saved on YouTube, so I turn the television on and find them, hitting play so I can get down to business. But even my favorite morning flow can't get the night before out of my head.

Duncan comes into my thoughts as I take a big breath in, letting it out of my mouth in a *whoosh*. Bending at the waist, I flatten my back and touch my toes, holding this position for a moment before rising up and reaching toward the sky. He's such a young boy, too young to attempt shoplifting, yet he did. At my bookstore.

And a cookbook? My internal monologue is blaming this one for wanting attention. Unless he plans to be a chef one day—and who knows? He could be—I can't see a ten-year-old stealing a cookbook for any other reason. He says it's a gift, but is it really?

Shaking my head, I order myself to let it go as the instructor on the screen moves into a downward dog. This is my time to clear my head and get ready for the day ahead. Toto could wake up at any moment, and he'll need a walk before I go to the shop.

Moving out of the downward dog into a front lunge, thankfully Duncan leaves my thoughts, but only for Levi to step in and take over. Poor guy. We texted and stayed in touch all during his regular playing season, but I've hardly seen him the last few months because he's been busy with his post-season commitments for his team as well as the brands he represents, the farm, the podcast he does with his brother, and of course, all the prep for getting Duncan settled in.

Levi is a wide receiver and plays for the Carolina Cardinals, our NFL team from North Carolina and the Super Bowl champions this year. Even with everything going on around him, he'd focused hard on making this a good year for his career. All the while knowing that once the season was over, he'd be taking over as guardian of this tiny thief.

I'd spent many a night on the phone with him when he was out of town for away games attempting to calm him down. He never admitted he was nervous, but I know that Duncan's grandmother makes him anxious. In the beginning, she appeared to be super kind and helpful. Because of the way things had happened so suddenly, an agreement was made so Levi could fulfill his work for the season while she kept

Duncan during that time. Levi would then move Duncan in with him during the off-season. This would give Levi time to do what he needed: get a room set up for Duncan, figure out school, all while playing for the Cardinals. He's going to need a plan for next year, one that shows he's around to help raise Duncan.

Changing sides, I take my left leg and put it in front of me into a lunge position and then rise up from my waist, reaching for the sky. All is quiet in my apartment, save the snoring dog hunkered down on his bed in the other room. So. Loud. I never knew a dog could snore with the impact of a freight train. Don't get me started on the slobber. It's so out of control, the dog shakes his head and you're covered, but Toto is my man and my protector. He can slobber all he wants.

I wrap up my workout in the next few minutes, not bothering to lie in Shavasana this time. I know in yoga practice they say that's the part you need to do because it's when all of the good stuff you just did for your body lands where it needs to, but I've got a dog to walk.

I flick on my coffee maker and then grab Toto's leash as I call out for him. It takes him a few moments, but soon he joins me in the kitchen, eyes sleepily squinting. Fastening his leash to his collar, I give him kisses on the tip top of his head while he grumbles a hello. It's our way of saying good morning.

I've got this walk timed so my coffee will be fresh and hot and waiting for me when I get back inside. Glancing at my watch, I know we have time. It's only a few minutes before seven. Smiling, I pat myself on the back. I'm glad I'd set my alarm early this morning.

I've barely made it onto Main Street when my phone rings. Unzipping the pocket of my running jacket, I pull it out, surprised to see Levi's name flashing on the screen.

"And what do I owe this early morning pleasure to?" I say when I answer.

"I didn't call too early, did I?" Levi's drawl is my own version of Southern comfort. It's one of the things I love most about being a transplant to these parts: the accent. Even when someone is telling you off, it sounds like a really sweet country song lyric.

"Why, no you didn't," I coo back in my best faux accent. I'm from the city, so of course I'm mesmerized. Probably always will be. "It's never too early for Levi Porter to call."

"Yet I think it is too early for you to try on that accent once again." He chuckles in my ear. "How long have you lived here, and you still haven't picked up even a trace of a Southern drawl?"

"I've been here for about four years now. And no, there's no Southern drawl. I love the accent, but a girl has to stay true to her roots."

"If you were doing that," Levi presses, "then why don't I hear your New *Yawker* accent any longer?"

"Because even my accent gets confused as to where I am and who I am," I manage to say with a laugh as Toto pulls me into a small park off the street. "What do you want anyway?"

A heavy sigh slams against my ear. "To say I'm so sorry again. I cannot believe that Duncan tried to lift a book from your shop."

"It's fine. He'll come in and work it off today. It'll be a lesson."

"But why did he have to do it to you?" I can hear the upset in his voice. "It's not the best way to start our new life together."

"Look, this is new for you. You're going to have moments like this where he's going to test the boundaries and you have to be prepared."

"When I was younger and I messed up, or if Austin did, our punishment was to go and work on our neighbour's farm."

"Why the neighbor's farm and not yours?"

"They have milking cows and need their manure pit cleaned out."

"Ewww." I giggle. "Then he needs to be told how lucky he is."

"That's the truth. It's not fun." When he goes silent, I let the line between us stay quiet. I've gotten to know him well enough that I know he's in thought, so I stay focused on the path in front of me and trot along after my dog, who has his nose in the air chasing some rogue smell or another.

"Thank you for being so cool about this," Levi murmurs as he finally breaks the silence. "I'm going to come in with Austin to drop him off. We need to check in on some of our rentals, plus there's a couple of properties we're thinking of buying in Sweetkiss Creek as investments. I'm trying to find a suitable home for Duncan and myself." Levi pauses, inhaling sharply. "But, I don't know. He's quiet, Georgie. The most he's spoken to me so far was last night when we were outside the bookstore."

I feel Levi's sadness like it's mine. The defeat in his voice isn't something I'm used to. "Well, today's a new day. And these things take time, right? He's been living with his grandmother and who knows what that was like for him."

"Lorna is not the easiest woman to be around, that much I remember from conversations I'd had with Tom and Katie over the years." There's a rustling sound as Levi moves around on his end of the line.

"Are you still in bed?" I ask.

"Yes. As a new parent, I need all of the rest I can sneak in, thank you." I'm fighting a laugh when there's a high-pitched shriek in my ear, almost like a mix between a squeak and a yelp, followed by a dull thud as the phone hits the ground. It's a brief but intense moment of chaos, a cacophony of noise followed by the clatter of it skidding across the floor before all noise abruptly ceases.

"What happened?" I manage as Levi comes back on the line. "Were you assaulted?"

"Yes, by Mom's cat." I hear a door slam and Levi breathes out on his end. "That stinking cat has been at my door all night."

"Aren't you allergic?" I'm trying not to laugh, but the octave of his squeal still reverberates in my head. If only Sports Center's hosts had heard it. It would be a viral sound to be used on TikTok over and over again by millions of viewers in a heartbeat.

"Very. But somehow this cat keeps getting inside at night and there's no other room, no other door, no other person it wants to hang out with. Just me."

"Of course. It's a cat."

What do you mean?"

"They can sense things. Like when someone doesn't like them."

"It's not that I don't like them, I think cats are awesome. I just can't let it get too close to me or I'll swell up like a balloon."

"How is he getting in?"

"It's a mystery. No one knows. Everyone swears it's not them and I can't find a way that he'd be sneaking in..."

"Like a tunnel? Or a trap door? Maybe the cat has a gang and they have a vault in the basement." Another thing about talking to Levi that makes me happy: I can be myself and there's just silliness. We can be serious, but he gets me when I'm just trying to make him laugh.

"And this is where you get ridiculous and I say goodbye," he says with a chuckle in my ear. My heart skips a beat; my job is done. "Before I go, I'm going to say I'm sorry again and thank you for letting him work off his misstep at your store. He'll be there at nine fifty-five exactly."

"See you guys then."

Disconnecting the call, I'm surprised that my cheeks are aching. I'm smiling that wide. This is what the man does to me.

Having a friend like Levi is the absolute best. To start with, he's the first guy I've met who listens to me—and asks questions. I know, shocking, right? If only I could clone him and date him. It's a thought I've had over the past year as I've struggled with my own feelings for this man.

Am I harboring a bit of a crush? Yes. I mean, the guy is HOT. He's like this Greek god who landed on earth and was put in this little town for all others to aspire to. And I'm being serious when I say that. From the moment I met him, I wanted to know more. He's one of those people who has a pull, a charm. Charisma that brings you into his orbit...if you're lucky enough, that is.

Have I dated other people while dealing with this crush? Yes. I've gone on a few dates over the past year and they all have been as exciting as clipping my toenails. Necessary, but not something I look forward to. Unless it's a spa pedicure, then sign me up. However, sadly, no man has ever been as good as that.

There was Dave, who I met on a dating app. He wouldn't stop talking when we went to dinner. He talked nonstop for over an hour and I was exhausted after. I usually have a backup plan when I go out on a first date like that, but I hadn't set anything up. You know, like phone-a-friend, a way out in case it turns out badly. I ended up going to the bathroom and setting my alarm on my phone. When it went off five minutes later, I pretended I was getting an emergency phone call so I could rush out the door and make my escape.

Of course, I can't forget DJ Luv, AKA Elton Clark. I met

him at a party in Charlotte; he was here from Vegas on vacation and recording an album. He came up to Sweetkiss Creek so we could go to dinner a few times, but we didn't click. For one thing, his day began at five p.m., when I was closing the store. His days were my nights, and we never found synchronicity in our schedules. Levi had a theory that if I really liked him, I'd have made it work, and he has a point. The night Elton asked me over a glass of wine how much I made in a year was probably the night I lost interest.

I've thought about putting a profile up on a dating app and also about trying a singles' night at one of the local bars in town, but no. In the end, I just can't do it.

So have I sworn off the dating scene? For the time being. I mean, Levi is back here for a few months, and I'd be lying to myself if I tried to ignore the fact that I want to, I don't know—see if we have a chance?

Toto and I make our way out of the park and back onto Main Street, navigating our way home. Passing by Altman's Furniture store, I peek in the window at the new items they have. There's a display showing off a new collection of pine furniture.

Pine. Pining.

Yes. That's what I am. I am pining for Levi Porter. I could almost make that into a poem: "Pathetically pining for a Porter" is what I'd call it.

Mr. Altman sees me staring through the glass as I walk by and he waves. He's always there early in the morning, before his staff. He's also a fan of autobiographies, and I usually keep a few behind the counter for him to check out when he stops in.

Coming from my own life issues, Sweetkiss Creek has been the second chance I never knew I'd need. So when I think about Levi and the ridiculous crush I have on him, I want to make my move slowly.

That's right, I'm going to make a move. He's been wrapped up with taking over guardianship and when he wasn't busy with that, he was on the road for work. Now that he's back, I'm really hoping I have a chance.

But first, there are other dragons to slay. Like a ten-year-old with a proclivity for lifting cookbooks.

FOUR

Levi

Opening the door to my bedroom, I follow the smell of coffee downstairs to the kitchen. Am I an adult male who lives at home on the farm with my family when I'm not traveling with my team? Why, yes, I am a proud card-carrying member of this exclusive club.

There's no other sound in the giant old farmhouse than the padding of my feet as I shuffle down the hallway. I like being here as much as I can and spending time with my mom. The Porter Family Farm is a working truffle farm; savory truffles, obviously, because who has a chocolate truffle farm besides Willy Wonka? It's one of the first to open its doors in North Carolina. My mother had started it years ago after my father had taken off and left her, literally, holding two babies in her arms. Me and my brother.

As I slowly push open the large wooden swinging door that leads into the kitchen, I pause when I hear low voices talking on the other side of it.

The sound of my mother's questioning tone hits my ears first. "So, do you want to help out in the field today, Duncan?"

I've got the door opened just a crack, my foot propping it at the bottom of its base, and there's a sliver of an opening where I can peek through and survey the room. Mom stands on one side, sipping her coffee and leaning against the sink while Duncan sits at the table, a bowl of cereal in front of him.

He shrugs his shoulders in response to her question. At least it's a two-shoulder shrug kind of day. When we brought him back here a few days ago, he'd barely lift anything or respond to us at all.

"Okay," Mom continues, never defeated. After what she's had to deal with in her life, I'm sure this small brick wall can't hold a candle to it. "There's always more shopping. I'm not sure if you have summer clothes or not, so I'll ask Levi if we can take inventory of your things and see if you want to go into town."

Duncan lifts his head but doesn't say anything still. I let my eyes bounce between him and my mother, wondering if she's thinking the same thing I am.

"We could also make ice cream if you'd like?" She offers this like a pacifier to a screaming child. Ever since she treated herself to this high-end ice cream maker, she thinks she's Ben or maybe it's Jerry. Not sure, but she's having a good time with it, even if Duncan is busy shaking his head from side to side, uninterested.

Not even the prospect of creating his own ice cream flavor gets this guy interested. How do we get through to this little man? Sighing, I drop my head. He's been through so much. At his age, he's already seen things that I could never comprehend, and here he is in our home. And we are strangers to him.

Steeling myself, I lift my head and push the door open.

"Good morning, everyone," I sing out, crossing the room to kiss Mom on her cheek. I pour my coffee and turn around, mimicking her stance against the counter. "So, what's going on in here?"

"We're trying to decide where the day will take us, right, Duncan?" Mom says, her gaze staying transfixed on the little man at her kitchen table. "There's a lot of possibilities."

"Well, Duncan already has plans for the day." Our eyes meet as he lifts a spoonful of something sugary and colorful to his lips. If he only knew how lucky he was to get my mom in grandmother mode, he wouldn't eat that cereal so slowly. When I was growing up, it was oatmeal or shredded wheat or eggs and toast. Only what Mom deemed to be healthy for us.

"Really?" Mom turns to face me, sipping her coffee.

"He's helping Georgie out at her shop today." Duncan's eyes slam into mine, a flash of worry behind them. I could rat him out to my mom, but I won't. He made his mistake. I can tell her about it later, but right now, I want to get him settled in here, and making him feel like a petty thief may not be the way to do it. "She needed a hand unloading some boxes, and Duncan really likes books, don't you, buddy?"

Duncan's big brown eyes darken slightly, little storm clouds swirling behind them. He turns his attention back to his cereal, lifting the spoon to his mouth and chewing.

"Speaking of books, Lorna dropped off a bag of them for Duncan last night while you were at dinner."

"Where is the bag?"

"I put it in the living room. There's a reading list for him, from school, and she's got information there on local camps he may be interested in going to while he settles into Sweetkiss Creek a little more."

"That's awesome," I say, keeping my voice light. Personally, I don't see where any good can come of sticking him into a summer camp after all he's been through, but what do I know? "Duncan, it's going to be a good summer. We'll get a routine down for you in no time, my friend."

Duncan doesn't acknowledge me one way or the other.

He simply lifts his spoonful of cereal to his mouth and chews, big brown eyes taking everything in.

Defeated, I look at my mother. She grabs the coffee pot and fills her mug, indicating for me to follow her as she heads to the back door.

"Levi, can I show you something in the yard real quick?"

I throw Duncan a smile and do as my mother tells me. As soon as I close the door behind me and walk onto the back porch, she grabs my hand and pulls me around to the side, where Duncan can't see us.

"That poor boy is still in a state of shock. We need to go really easy with him."

Now it's time to rat him out. "That poor boy is working at Georgie's today because she caught him trying to steal a book."

"What?" she snaps.

"You heard me right. He also spoke more last night than he has in the short amount of time he's been with us."

My mother's eyebrows arch in surprise. "He did?"

"Only when he was trying to explain himself." I put a hand on my hip. "Georgie said he could come and work it off today. Which is better than the fact she could have pressed charges."

Mom turns and leans on the porch railing, looking over the backyard as she grips onto her mug so tight her knuckles turn white. She's raised two boys, she knows how they can be, but I'm sure this kind of thing is a bit of a surprise. No one expects to have a small human around who likes to lift things.

"We're lucky it's Georgie and she's a kind soul. What was he thinking?"

"I'd love to know," I say with a heavy sigh, leaning against the railing and once again, mimicking my mother's stance. I follow her line of sight to where Austin, my younger brother, stands out in one of the fields. Four dogs bounce around him, playing. "But it's not like he's opening up to me, is it?"

"With time, sweetie. He had to get used to all of this change. He's had a lot handed to him."

She's right. I know I'm still coming to grips with what's happened and the loss. Tom was my high school best friend and we'd stayed the kind of friends over the years who, no matter what, could pick things up where we left them. It was always like no time had passed when we got together. No matter where our lives took us, we had our growing up in common.

There'd been a fire at their house, and luckily Duncan made it out. His parents, sadly, weren't so lucky. Katie passed away immediately from inhalation, and we had all hoped and prayed that Tom would make it through. I'd flown to New York and stayed with Duncan, while Tom was kept in a coma.

When Tom passed away, I brought Duncan back to Sweetkiss Creek with me, but I was about to start my season, with a contract that wouldn't allow any time away to help get Duncan settled. Quick to raise her hand to help, Lorna all but insisted she take Duncan for the time being.

However, at the end of my season, Duncan was still settling into his new life. When Lorna brought up the fact it could be better for his mental health, and for consistency, that he stay with her at least until the school year was over, I was hesitant. But, I said yes. Cause it's about Duncan and his needs, not what I want. He was barely speaking and wasn't communicating with anyone, not even with Lorna. I'd encouraged her to seek help from a therapist, but she didn't think it was needed. Her words to me were that he'd come around, she was his grandmother after all, so she'd get him talking.

But she didn't—and he isn't.

"You're right. I think it's time I made an appointment for him to see a therapist," I say, turning to the side, angling myself to face her. "We can't begin to understand what he's been through, and I don't know anyone he can talk to that could be a sounding board who would 'get it.' It's time for the professionals to help us out."

"I can do some research today and see who I can find locally," she says, knowingly, nodding her head in agreement. "He'll come out of his shell eventually. We just have to be patient."

I nod in understanding. As I do, Mom nudges me in the ribs with her elbow. "So, if he was at Pages and Prose 'shopping,'" she says using air quotes, "does that mean you saw Georgie last night?"

"Aren't you subtle?" I laugh. "Yes, I saw her last night."

"Can't stay away, can you?"

"What's that supposed to mean?"

"Exactly what I said. You and your good friend, your 'girlfriend,'" she says, making use of those air quotes once again, "make a cute couple, you know."

I can feel the heat of embarrassment in my cheeks. "She is my friend. Not my girlfriend."

"She is a girl who is your friend." She holds her mug in the air, punctuating her words. "Therefore a girlfriend."

"I'm not going to argue with you about this."

A voice pipes up behind us. "Who's arguing and what's it about?"

Spinning on my heel, I turn around and find Austin standing on the porch with his hands over his eyes, shielding them from the sun.

"How did you get up here so fast?" I ask, pointing back to the fields. "You were just out there."

"I can move quickly when I want to, big brother. Better than you some days. Probs why my contract has already been extended for next year," he says, a teasing lilt to his voice. My brother also plays in the NFL, he's a tight end, but for one of my opposing teams, the Tampa Bay Thunderbolts. "How's Duncan today?"

I shrug. "The same."

Austin walks over and pats my shoulder before throwing himself into one of the Adirondack chairs on the porch. "Once he gets used to us, to this place, he'll come around."

"I hope so," I say, parking in a chair beside him. "But in the meantime, where do we go from here?"

"What do you mean?" Mom asks, tilting her to one side.

"I think in order to quell any issues Lorna may have, I need to put some plans into motion that show I'm serious about taking care of him. Show her, visibly somehow, that I'm prepared to be a more present figure in his life."

"Dude, you were taken by surprise last year and you guys really did need to go slow to make sure you didn't rock his foundation more than it was already. What else can you do?" Austin queries, his eyes narrowing with understanding. "Wait. You're not thinking of moving are you?"

I nod my head slowly. "I am. I think getting a place that is just his and mine would be a good start."

"What about playing football?" Austin asks as I shrug.

"Don't know right now. I've not signed anything because..." I throw my hands in the air. "I need to make a decision based on what's best for Duncan. That may mean it's time to step down from the team."

"But have you—"

I hold up a hand to cut him off. "I'm not prepared to talk about it right now, but I will. When I have time to think about what I want to do and see what's best for Duncan, then I'll know."

I knew Austin would have an opinion about this, and I half-expected my brother's reaction to be bigger, like he'd want to talk me out of stepping away from football, but instead he nods his head in silent understanding. "I get it, but does it really mean you need to leave the farm?"

"What your brother said. I understand why you're rethinking your career, but we're your family." My mother doesn't even try to hide her disappointment. "If you're here, we can chip in and help."

"I know, but there has to be some independence in it." I look around the farmland surrounding the house. "We're not that close to Sweetkiss Creek, and I think it may be good for him to have more stimulation as he gets used to being here. He wasn't communicative while at Lorna's, but he did seem to like living in town."

"He's a city boy, grew up in New York, right?" Austin asks as I nod.

"Well, I don't see why the farm would be a bad palace for him to be," Mom huffs my way, disgruntled.

"I want him to come out here to the farm. I think living out here is the best thing ever, but maybe we live in town for a year or two first so he can make friends and have easy access to things, like he did in New York."

"He could also get in trouble." Mom glances at Austin. "Georgie caught him shoplifting in her store last night."

As Austin's eyes widen, I groan. "Mom. I don't want everyone knowing about this. It'll embarrass him."

"Maybe he needs to be." Austin chuckles. "What kind of book did he take anyway? I bet it was the Victoria's Secret anniversary edition of their top runway looks over the years..."

I roll my eyes. My brother, all class. "A cookbook."

"That's not even interesting." Austin snickers. "How did your girlfriend handle it?"

"She's not my girlfriend," I whine. These two won't let up. The fact that I really like Georgie aside, I don't need nor want to be teased right now. "And she's got him coming in to do physical labor today to teach him a lesson. Speaking of which..." I glance at my watch. "I should get a shower and get ready to take him in."

Austin rises from his seat, patting my shoulder as he walks by. "Give me a few minutes and I'll be ready to go."

We watch as he goes back inside, leaving me alone with our mother again.

"That's a lot you just shared. Moving away from here and considering not going back to play?" She puts her mug on the railing of the deck and crosses her arms. "Have you really thought about all of this and what it means?"

I nod. "I've done nothing but think about it, over and over. Not having Dad around when I was little meant you had to sign us up for Big Brothers Big Sisters. You did as much as you could, putting us first. I want to be the same. I want to show up for him."

"But that doesn't mean you have to quit doing something you love," she says, cocking her head to one side as she takes me in. "You still love playing football, right?"

I look down at my hand, where my Super Bowl ring sits on the days I choose to get it out and wear it. "That's a question I've asked myself a lot lately. What do I love and what do I have passion for?" I scratch the top of my head. "I guess I've not had a chance to really check in with myself over it and still need to."

"Fair enough," she says as she nods toward the house. "I'm going to get the kid motivated to get out, and you need to get some breakfast in your body before you guys leave. You may be an adult, but I can still tell you what to do."

I laugh as she walks back inside, leaving me on the deck thinking about football and my future.

I can see a future where I'm not at practice and not having to put my body through so much work. I want a future where I'm present for this kid, doing what Tom and Katie would have wanted me to do. Be a parent.

I'd love a future where that kid gets the best of both worlds and can be with me and have a relationship with his grandmother, and where I'm not in fear Lorna will try to get him and take him from me.

But mostly, I want a future with one particular bookstore-owning woman by my side.

FIVE

Georgie

Reaching for my second cup of coffee for the day, I keep one eye on the kid, who is currently paying his penance for his attempt at thievery last night. I don't think any other shop owners on this street would have been as cool as I was. Since most of them are older and have been in Sweetkiss for all their lives, I'd venture as far as to say that they're stuck in their ways and would have had Zac arrest him, done something a bit more extreme.

But that just is not who I am.

I pat myself on the back for being a bit more realistic about the situation and adaptable. I don't talk about my past very often, not that it comes up in conversation, but I was a foster kid. That meant being shuffled from house to house when I was younger, though I got used to it. There was always a moment of sadness when I had to pack and unpack again, for the first time or two at least, but then I made it into a game.

I had to learn to be independent when I was younger out of sheer protection for myself and my wellbeing, and it's a trait

I've carried with me into adulthood. I don't consider it toxic, instead I say it's one of my best qualities. Now, did I ever resort to stealing? No. But did I consider it when I was at school and everyone else had shiny new Christmas or birthday gifts and I didn't? Yeah. I did. I said I was adaptable, not a perfect angel.

Duncan kneels on the floor on the other side of the counter, pulling a shipment of books out of a box and stacking them by the cash register. Me, I've parked myself on my stool behind the counter and I'm cracking my proverbial whip.

As he places another book on top of the pile that's growing, I put my coffee cup on the counter and point to the stack. Here comes that whip.

Turning to him, I put him in my sights. "So, Duncan, what do we do next?" *Thwack.*

Duncan's big brown eyes meet mine as he shrugs in that awesome way that only kids can do, where a shrug speaks volumes. "I dunno."

"Duncan," I say in my best adult-in-charge voice, threading my arms across my chest tightly. I also really like his name and enjoy saying it. "I just told you the steps to doing this. You know what to do." *Thwackity thwack.*

Duncan sighs, pushing his hair out of his face. I've watched him do that so many times today already, and it's only been about an hour that he's been here. The kid needs a hair tie or a haircut.

"I'm going to price the books, then put them on the table for the book signing."

"Yes!" I exclaim, slamming my hand on the counter with such force that it causes him to jump. "Sorry, I didn't mean to be so aggressive."

He bends down and grabs the now-empty box, handing it to me with an air of nonchalance. "I wasn't scared."

I purse my lips together super tight, trying with all of my might to keep this smile from creeping across my face as it threatens to literally explode into my cheeks. "You're funny."

Duncan cocks his head to one side and looks at me like I'm suddenly holding something really weird. Like a chicken or an octopus. "What do you mean?"

I can read people. Like, in an empathetic way. I had someone tell me once that my empathy volume is turned all the way up and that it must be hard for me sometimes because of all the feelings I catch, and I gotta say—they're so right. I can feel a room and its energy the moment I walk into it, and I can even vibe off the people as well. The emotion of a space can drip with weight and it affects us, as humans, and we don't even realize it. Well, I do, but it took me a long time to understand and hone that skill.

I look at Duncan knowingly. "What I mean is that you're funny in the way that I can see through you."

"You can see through me?" He rolls his eyes. "Lady, I'm not a ghost."

I purse my lips and give him a librarian-like *tsk*. "Lady?"

"Sorry," he says automatically. "Ma'am?"

I stifle the laughter bubbling inside. He's witty, but I'm not going to let him know that either. As a former defensive child myself, of course I get him. But I know I need to also play this slowly so I don't scare him off. I know from all of my late-night talks with Levi that Duncan's had a rough time mourning the loss of his parents, and I cannot even begin to imagine where his head is, even with my empath skills.

I tap on the counter, keeping my gaze level with his, before deciding to move on. I don't want him to know I've got his number. Yet.

"You're right. You're not a ghost, something you proved to us last night when you tried to steal that book." I hop off the stool, kicking it behind me as I point down an aisle, toward the back of the store. "All of these books here are on special so they need to be priced using my sales sheet. What doesn't go on the table will then be stacked in the spot on the shelves that's been cleared." I thrust a piece of paper, the aforementioned sales sheet, his way. "Go by this sheet, then go stack, then let me know it's done and I'll double-check your work."

He doesn't say anything, he just huffs. It's a weighted huff, filled with a few unsaid expletives, but I refuse to be moved by his attitude. He won't break me. I watch as he snatches up the sales sheet and studies it, my phone going off in my bag beside me.

Figuring it's probably Levi, I don't even look at the screen to check. I press the phone to my ear. "¡Hola! ¿Cómo estás?"

There's silence on the other end. After a few seconds, someone clears their throat. "Is this Georgina Simpson? From Apartment 2 at 313 West Third Street?"

My full name being used is always a cause for concern. "Yeeeessss," I answer, slowly dragging that word out as long as I can. My confidence has just gone south. "Can I help you?"

"This is Loretta Steele. I work for the rental company that handles your building. I'm not sure if you're aware, but we were there earlier this week doing a yearly inspection."

I vaguely remember seeing a note in my mailbox about this, but since I'm usually at the bookshop all day long, I didn't pay any attention.

"Sure. Is there something wrong with my apartment?"

"Not necessarily your apartment. It's more like the whole building. We'd had a report from one of your neighbors about termites."

Ew. Just the thought makes me shudder. Bugs of any kind, really. Don't even get me started on cockroaches.

"Okay," I say, making my way around the counter and meandering to the front of the shop, where the window overlooks the street. "Were there issues?"

Loretta sighs. "Yes, unfortunately, there's structural damage that we need to address as soon as we can."

"Structural damage?" That sounds ominous. My mind goes to an image of my giant Rottweiler sitting in my living room with the floor giving out, and suddenly, like a cartoon, the floor gives way and he's sitting in the middle of the giant basement that's below us. "How bad is it?"

"It's...not good. Look, we're required to give everyone seven days' notice to evacuate. We need to fumigate, then look at the damage that's been done and see if we are going to be able to fix it."

"So we need to leave temporarily?" Fingers crossed.

"Weeelll," she says, a little too high-pitched for my taste. "That's the thing. We don't know."

"You don't know?"

"No. It'll be like peeling an onion. We need to check out the layers."

A sick feeling hits my stomach. "Do I need to pack my things and box them up, as if I'm moving out?"

"It's advisable."

This woman is going to make me scream. "Loretta, I need you to understand I'm a single woman who owns her own business. I have a dog, and that's it. It's just us. But I need to know what kind of long-term plan I may need to consider."

"I shouldn't be telling you this, but there's a possibility you could be out of your apartment for up to three months or more."

"So I need to move?" Now my voice is taking on a high-pitched tone that makes me cringe. I've seriously hit an octave that could rival an opera singer.

"I'm not going to say that, but I will say you should think about other options," she whispers. "From one single woman to another, you gotta take care of you."

I get the gist of what she's saying even though I wish I didn't. "When do we need to be out?"

"Well, like I said, you have seven days to evacuate. Legally, we have up to four days to fumigate and then another four business days to inspect the structure."

"So I'm out of my house for at least eight days?"

"We go by 'business days,' so really closer to two weeks."

This is getting sticky and messy. Fast. "So, I need to find a place that will take me and my dog, and I have seven days to do it?" A noise behind me startles me, causing me to turn. I'd forgotten momentarily about Duncan being here until I see him standing at the counter giving me a thumbs-up.

"We'll organize some compensation for accommodation, and I'll see if there is anything else you have a right to as a tenant." She pauses, and I can picture Loretta on her end of the phone: she has glasses in my version of her, they're wire-rimmed and cat-like, and her hair is jet black and pulled back into a tight bun. Matronly but also kind, yet a hint of scary. "I know this is distressing and sudden, and I'm so sorry. I hate being the bearer of bad news, but look...I just work here."

Way to wiggle out of any accountability. Now where do I direct my anger? "I hear ya, Loretta. Thank you for the call?" I roll my eyes as the words fall out of my mouth. There's nothing to be thankful about here. Nothing.

I'd had a hard time finding a place to rent that would take dogs, much less a Rottie as big as mine. Toto is a giant baby doll, but tell that to the average Joe walking down the street. Landlords see a dog his size and automatically think "She has no control over him," yet they have no idea how much training that dog, and I, have been through.

Disconnecting the call, I shove my phone in my back pocket and plaster a smile on my face as I walk back up to the counter. I can feel Duncan's eyes watching me carefully, so I make a show out of checking my watch for the time.

"Okay, your time here is almost done, my friend. Levi is going to be here to pick you up in a half hour, so let's look at your work." I reach behind the counter, grab the cookbook he'd tried to steal the night before, and slide it across the counter. "Obviously, this is payment today."

Duncan looks at the cookbook, then drags his eyes to mine. "Do you have to move out of your house?"

Kids. I forget they hear everything.

I nod my head, then shake it as I shrug my shoulders. I'm a mess, but I try to play it cool. After all, I'm the adult here, so he can't see me sweat. "I dunno? Maybe. We'll see."

"You have a dog?"

Smiling, I pull my phone out and show him the picture of me and Toto that I use as my lock screen image. "This is my baby boy."

"Oh...WOW." Duncan laughs, taking the phone from my hands. "He's big!"

"He really is." I giggle. "Maybe you can meet one day."

"Yeah," Duncan says, his eyes sliding back over to the cookbook. "So, I get to have that now?"

"You earned it."

He pulls it across the counter and flips it open, smiling as he looks at the pages. "Thank you."

"Of course." We stand quietly for a few minutes, him thumbing the pages, me staring as he does and thinking about my impending homelessness. "Do you want to tell me why that particular cookbook is the one you wanted?"

I'd be a fool to not see his face cloud over; it's as if a dark storm cloud has entered the vicinity and is only hanging out above Duncan. His eyes flicker as they look around the room, like he's batting back tears. I stay still, not wanting to disturb his thought process, but we're both startled when the bell above the door rings out as a customer comes inside.

When I turn to greet them, part of me is a little surprised

to see Levi with Austin on his heels. Grinning from ear to ear, he holds up a couple of giant to-go cups and shakes them in the air.

"I brought you guys Georgie's favorite. Fresh squeezed lemonade." He hands me one before turning to Duncan and handing him his. "From my mom to you. How's it been going?"

"I was just about to look at Duncan's work. He set up the table and display for the book signing this week, and"—I pat the cookbook that still rests on the counter in front of him—"he earned his book, didn't you?"

Eyes on the floor, Duncan shrugs as he turns away from us, putting his back to Levi. Cocking my head to one side, Levi and I exchange a look. I can see in his eyes there's some confusion, and I'm beginning to understand even more. This is not the kid I've been hanging out with the last few hours.

"Dude, we need to make our next appointment," Austin interrupts, giving me a wave. "Hey, Georgie."

"Hi, Austin." I grab a bag from behind the counter and slide the cookbook inside it, turning it over to Duncan and leaning down to talk to him so only he can hear me. I can sense he's hesitant, and while I want to reassure him, I also want to make sure that what he heard about my housing issue doesn't become a topic of conversation with the Porters. "This is yours. Anything we say, me or you, when you're here, that's for us to know. I hereby deem this our safe space, capiche?"

Holding out my hand, I stick out my pinky. I'm going full-on pinky swear here and luckily Duncan is a fan of this as well. Chewing back a small smile, he wraps his pinky in mine and nods his head once.

"Okay, then." Standing up straight once more, I wink at Levi. "He's dismissed."

Austin waits for Duncan to join him, and with a wave, the

pair disappear from our sight. Levi, who had been standing with his perfect posture looking quite self-assured, suddenly folds in on himself, collapsing onto the counter and putting his head in his hands.

"He hates me, Georgie."

"I wouldn't say hate, that's a strong emotion."

"He does. He hardly talks to any of us."

I lean against the checkout counter. "Really?"

"You sound surprised," his voice oozing with defeat as he glances my way.

"He's been here talking to me all morning."

"Stop it." Levi shakes his head. "About what?"

"I don't know. Books, Toto, nothing major. Just talking."

Levi stares at me incredulously. "Are you serious?"

"Yes," I say, noticing he now looks a little...bummed.

"So Duncan talks to you."

"It's not like I'm anything special, I'm just the adult who doesn't know his whole story, at least in his eyes. Maybe you guys are too close?"

Levi opens his mouth to say something, but instead chooses to shrug as his phone chimes. Reaching into his back pocket, he slides it out and his face goes pale. Like ghostly-white pale right in front of me. You know the saying that someone's had the blood drained from their face? Yep. Like a vampire is actually sucking his life force out of him in front of me.

"You okay?"

"It's my mom. I need to go now." Turning on his heel, he heads for the exit, but turns around as he grips the handle. "Thank you, again, for going easy on him."

"Of course, I wouldn't have it any other way."

With one last wave, Levi sprints out to the waiting SUV and climbs in the back seat. Austin is behind the wheel with

Duncan sitting in the front seat beside him, giving me a small wave as they tear off down the street.

And leaving me to wonder if I'll ever feel like I can step up and be woman enough for Levi Porter or not.

SIX

Levi

"The sheriff delivered them himself?" I hold a pile of paperwork in my hands, waving it in the air. I know I must look like a madman, but I can't help it. I'm furious. Spitting tacks angry. In the mood to burn something, or someone, down, and we'll call her Lorna. "How could she do this?"

My mother and Austin have been listening to me rant for the past ten minutes. I'm pretty sure I've paced the floor of this converted barn to the point there's a ditch beneath my feet.

"Levi, take a breath for a second—"

"It's messed up, Ma," Austin chimes in. "She agreed with him they should do Duncan's custody this way."

"It's the way Tom and Katie wanted it to be," I interject. The interrupter is now talking over the interrupter. "They asked me to be his godfather and they took that seriously enough they made me his guardian if anything ever happened to them. She has to see that in the eyes of the law, and her son, I'm the one he's supposed to be with."

"I'm not trying to argue the point with you, I just want to

keep you from being so stressed out." She walks over from where she's been standing in the doorway of our renovated barn, keeping an eye out to make sure Duncan didn't accidentally walk in on us discussing him or hear us talking about his grandmother.

Sighing as she collapses into one of the oversized and overstuffed bean bags we have scattered about, she closes her eyes and lays her head back, staring at a row of plants hanging from planters that swing on exposed beams above. "Why can't we just have a smooth run of things? Why can't we just raise that sweet boy in peace?"

"This is not the kind of thing that will help him. He barely speaks now," Austin says as he gets up from behind his desk and walks over to the fridge, pulling out three bottles of beer. He flicks the tops off and walks around, handing one to my mother and me and keeping one for himself.

"Barely speaks to us. Or to his grandmother," I say, taking a sip of the cold brew. "But, he talks to Georgie."

"I've tried to bribe that boy with everything. Including my ice cream." Mom crosses her arms and hones in on me. "What do they talk about—did you ask her?"

I nod. "Nothing, really. When I picked him up today she mentioned they'd chatted again, but since he was working at her store, you'd think he would."

"He kind of spoke to me today," Austin chimes in. "You were still inside the bookstore. When I asked if he'd like to go back to help Georgie sometime."

I stare at Austin with disbelief. "And?"

Austin shrugs his shoulders. "He said yes."

"That's all?" I ask, fighting the instantaneous urge I have to roll my eyes. Putting the paperwork down, I rake my fingers through my hair, massaging my scalp in an attempt to keep the headache that's sure to come at bay.

Austin nods, his eyes sliding over to my mother and

exchanging a look. Like a silent request for permission. Judging by the glare my mother is giving him, the answer is no, but that doesn't stop my brother.

"What's that look for?" I ask, pointing to the two of them, my finger swaying back and forth in the wind. "That. That look."

"Well, maybe raising a ten-year-old isn't the thing you should be doing right now, Levi," Austin says, his voice low.

A bubble of irritation wells in my chest, followed by a crack of pain so sharp I'm pretty sure I am about to have a heart attack. It passes quickly, but I'm certain it's added fuel to my fire.

"That is so easy for you to say, isn't it?" I take another swig of my beer, placing the bottle on the ping-pong table before I lean on it to stabilize myself. I feel like a kite without a string and I don't want to come unhinged right now. "You're not the one who was asked to take care of him, Austin. I was."

Austin holds his hands up in surrender. "Dude. I'm not against you; I simply want to remind you that life could be different. Maybe you don't have to be a stand-in father for Duncan. It could be better if he goes to live with his grand-mother, you know?"

He angles himself to look at my mother, raising his hands in the air even higher. "Please back me up here and tell him I have a point?"

"Of course you do," she acquiesces. "However, that's your opinion. This is up to Levi, honey, not us."

"It's not even up to Levi anymore, is it?" I say, talking about myself in the third person and standing up tall and swiping at the paper again, whipping it off the table to scan it once more. "It's up to the courts to decide if I'm going to be a good enough—what do you call it, Austin? Stand-in parent? —to take care of Duncan."

"I didn't mean it to upset you," he says, rising from his

seat. Austin's tone is apologetic, but I'm looking for a scapegoat. "I'm playing devil's advocate. I wish I could unsay it."

"But you said it." I grab a stray ping-pong ball and start bouncing it on the table. "And that's something we can't do while there's a ten-year-old kid running around here, is it? We can't go off and say what we think."

"We've always had an open convo policy in our family," my mother intervenes, her eyes focused on me, watching as I bounce this silly ball. It sounds somewhat soothing. *Patink, patink, patink.* There's a cadence as I let it go, watch it connect with the table, and then grab it again out of the air. *Patink, patink, patink.*

"Your brother only wanted to tell you what he thinks, Levi, so don't silence him because it's not what you want to hear," she continues, her eyes following the ball. "Right now, you need to be open to all options because it's kind of out of your hands."

"I'm going to get a lawyer." *Patink, patink, patink.*

"Of course you will, and I'll help you find them. In fact..." Austin scurries to the other side of his desk, opening his laptop. "I'll pull up some names now."

"I can do it myself." *Patink, patink, patink.*

There's a rustling sound as my mother attempts to rise from the beanbag. It's over-stuffed and oversized, remember, so it likes to eat those who even dare to rest on it. I watch her struggle in my periphery for only a moment before I finally chuck the stinking ball against the wall on the other side of the room, vindicated by the smack it makes when it hits, and offer my hand to pull her out of what must feel like bean-filled quicksand.

"I was wondering if either one of you would come help me," she says with a chuckle, wrapping an arm around my shoulders. "Look, you need to calm down. I don't know what you have to do to find some solace right now, but I'm going to kick you out of here while you find it."

"What?"

"You heard me. You're in shock from being served, we all are, and it stings. The past year has been one shock after another, one life change too many in my opinion, but we'll handle it." She makes a sweeping motion with her hands that encompasses the room. "All of us—Duncan, too—we'll handle it as a family. But you need to calm down fast. You're the father figure now. That boy"—she points toward the barn door —"the one playing video games and not engaging with us, needs an adult who has got his back, okay? He needs someone who is gonna show him how to be a good man. A strong and patient and kind man. I cannot think of anyone else who is better for that job, in the absence of Tom, than you."

I let her words wash over me, letting them sink in fully. Slowly I nod my head. "You're right."

"Did I hear you correctly? Is my son admitting his mother is right?" she asks, teasing back in her tone and a slight smile beginning to play on her lips.

"Yes. I'm admitting you're right. You're a mom after all; I think you've got an idea of what this job entails."

"Good point," she says, kissing my cheek. "Now, go. I don't care where it is, just go to it and come back later. After dinner, preferably."

"But, Duncan..."

"Can hang out with me," Austin calls out. "I want to run the dogs, so we'll go out in the fields and down to the river. There's something peaceful about that place and he may dig it."

"When you're back, I'll make us ice cream sundaes," Mom begins, then sees Austin and me catch each other's eye and make faces. "Stop that. I see you. You'll eat my ice cream and you'll enjoy every bite of it. Then, we'll talk about a lawyer and next steps, but that doesn't have to be tonight. We can do it tomorrow." Mom points to where my keys still sit on the desk where I'd tossed them when I came in earlier. "Go."

Nodding, I do as I'm told, if for no other reason than to stop her from talking about her ice cream. We're a mere mention away from her opening her own ice cream parlor.

I cross the barn floor in a few long strides, turning around as I slide the giant door open to go. Mom's already standing behind Austin, peering over his shoulder at the laptop and pointing to what he sees.

"That's a good list. Bring that thing down to the house where we'll be closer to Duncan," she commands.

"Yeah, he's been playing that video game long enough," I add, but my offering is met by the glare of two sets of eyes.

"Go," my mother repeats, pointing to the world beyond the barn door. "Now."

Austin can't hide his delight at my being scolded, and even though I'm madder than I've been in a long time, it makes me grin. This is family. Coming together for a common goal. I love them, they love me. I want to give this to Duncan. Tom saw something in me, in my family, that he trusted me enough to give this to his son. I have to honor that.

Climbing into my SUV, my mind is blank and whirling all at the same time. Turning the keys in the ignition, I let the car warm up as I let out a giant breath of air.

I don't know where to go, yet there's only one place I can think of that I want to be right now and only one person I really want to talk to.

However, there's someone else I need to go see first.

SEVEN

Levi

In the fun way small towns work, of course I called our family lawyer and asked if I could stop by to get his advice on something. Did you think I was going to sit here and be served papers by Lorna quietly?

Buzz Sherman has been our lawyer and family friend for as long as I can remember. When everything went down last year and I found out about being Duncan's guardian, I'd asked him to look over all the paperwork and to be available in case I needed him. Look, this is the first time I've been "willed" something, and for it to be a human life, I want to make sure I do it right.

When I turned into Buzz's driveway in town, he was already sitting on his porch waiting for me. He always reminded us of Santa Claus growing up—in fact, one year, Mom had him come out to the farm and play Santa for Austin and me, as well as for his two kids, who are both grown and gone now. I think one went to Los Angeles and is now a lawyer, too, following in his father's shoes. The other owns a taco stand somewhere in the Florida Keys. It's like he couldn't have two more different kids if he tried.

"Thanks for seeing me on such short notice, Buzz," I call out, slamming my car door and walking across the lawn.

"Anything for you kids. You know that you and your mom mean the world to us." He stands, indicating I follow him inside.

The old Victorian home sits on the edge of Sweetkiss Creek Park, one of the best spots to live in my opinion if you're going to dwell here in town. You get the benefit of a green space across the street from your front yard, and you're still a quick walk into the shopping district if you want to do anything or grab a bite to eat.

We settle in his study, Buzz taking a chair across from me, grabbing a legal pad and a pen. "May I see the papers you were served?" he asks. I comply, handing them over and then I settle in to wait for him to review them.

It feels like ages, but he finally grunts his dissatisfaction.

"Well, she's going to try to make things difficult for you, isn't she?" Buzz angles himself in his chair so he's facing me. It's late afternoon now and the sun is starting to get lower in the sky, but it hasn't started to disappear yet. Its warmth still emanates enough heat that I can feel it through the window panes sitting here in Buzz's study.

"I guess so. I mean, I know she wasn't happy that I was chosen to be guardian, but…" I shake my head and run my fingers through my hair. "I don't know what to do, Buzz. He needs to settle in and something like this could ruin the work we're trying to do to help him."

"No, I get it. Mary told me about Duncan. I know he's a bit quiet and still in some shock, as I'm sure you can understand." Buzz's features are soft, but his mouth is drawn in a tight line. "I hate these cases because the child can quickly feel like property."

"I don't want that," I offer.

Buzz reaches out to pat my shoulder. "I know, I wasn't

talking about you," he says knowingly. "This can go a couple of ways, depending on the judge you get, really. They could try to show you as unfit to be his guardian because of the amount of time you're on the road for football."

I'd wondered if that was going to be a problem. "Doesn't it count that it's the way I make money and I'll be able to provide for Duncan by doing my job?" Tom and Katie had also left him a sizable trust fund which he'll be able to access when he's old enough, and provisions while he's under my care so he never has to want for anything, but still. If I'm going to be a dad, I'm going to be a dad, you know?

"Funny enough, because you're single, that could hurt you. Doesn't matter that your family is tight and your mom or brother can step in at any time, nor that you're making a decent salary in the NFL. Duncan's grandmother may try to show you as unfit."

"This is insane, right?" Folding my arms in front of me, I can't help but to throw myself back into the chair with a little anger, to the point the chair rocks for a second before it stops and stays still.

"You need to breathe, son," Buzz says in his soft Southern drawl. "I'd offer you a whiskey, but since you're driving, a Cheerwine seems more appropriate."

Cheerwine. The best cherry-flavored soft drink ever. "Yes, please."

Buzz leans forward and picks up his desk phone and hits a button. Someone on the other end picks up and he rattles off an order: a glass of ice, Cheerwine times two, and a couple of Moon Pies.

Grinning, he turns back to me. "Those were always the best comfort foods for our family. I figure we could both use 'em right now."

"Thanks, Buzz," I say, my shoulders shaking with a small laugh. "What else do I need to be prepared for?"

"Well, they'll look at you—not just look, but their lawyers will scrutinize everything you do and bring that with them to court. They'll want...no, *need*, to prove that you're unfit because the law doesn't favor a grandparent in cases like this. Not when the parents have assigned guardianship and laid it out in a will."

"So I should, by all rights, be able to win this?"

"Not necessarily. Like I said, it depends on the judge you get and the case made by their lawyer."

The study door creaks open, and a guy in his mid-twenties enters with our comfort items on a tray. He places everything down on the coffee table in front of us and leaves as stealthily as he entered.

"New intern," Buzz says. "He's working here a few hours a week for college credit."

Buzz has always had a great reputation as a family friend, but as a lawyer, he is the man. The guy you do not want to see up against you when you walk into a court of law, which has always boded well for us in the times we've needed him most.

"He's got a good teacher," I say as I grab my Cheerwine and crack it open, pouring it over ice.

"Here's to that," Buzz says, holding his can in the air as we clink them. "So, when you know who your judge is we can make a plan, but for now you need to do things that show you are currently, and plan to be in the future, an active member of Duncan's day-to-day life."

"How can I do that when I'm on the road starting in August or September?" My coaches are aware of this very new situation and I know I'll get some grace as we go into the new season, but this is starting to stress me out.

"Are you planning on still playing football?"

If he only knew how weighted that question was these days. "At the moment, it's unclear. I'm processing things."

Buzz nods in understanding. "Okay, let's go on the basis

that you stay playing pro ball. Get your family involved—your brother, mother. Your girlfriend?" The last part of the sentence comes out as a question, with Buzz's hopeful eyes honing in on me.

"Girlfriend?"

"Or fiancée?"

"Fiancée?" Laughing, I shake my head and put down my drink, grabbing for the Moon Pie. I need the chocolatey goodness of marshmallow and graham cracker in my belly right now for this topic. I'm a guy who is not ashamed of the fact that he can eat his feelings. "How did I go from girlfriend to fiancée in a matter of two ticks?"

"Let's be honest here," Buzz says, sitting back in his chair as he peels open the wrapper encasing his Moon Pie. "It'll look good to the courts if you're showing signs of settling down. Showing plans to get married and provide Duncan with a family."

"But," I manage with my mouth full, "I have a family. My mom and my brother. No one questioned us when my dad left, did they?"

"Different circumstances, Levi. She's your maternal momma. She had you, so she has rights. She is blood. You're...not."

That is obviously not what I want to hear, and I'm pretty sure it's evidenced by the look on my face.

"What's that look for?" Buzz inquires, raising his Moon Pie in the air. "'Cause in our house you can't be in a bad mood with a Moon Pie."

"It's unfair. I'm the one Tom and Katie wanted Duncan to be with, whatever their reasons were, and to think that his grandmother could come along and take that custody from me is nuts."

"If you really want to do this, to step up and be a dad to

this boy and help guide him, then you may need to do things so it looks as if."

As Buzz puts his soda to his lips and eyes me, I let his words resonate. "As if?"

He nods, taking a swig. I wait for him to gather his thoughts and speak again.

"Unofficially, I'm going to give you the best advice I can because I love you guys and I consider the Porters to be family." His face suddenly turns serious as he leans forward and sets his drink on the coffee table, placing the Moon Pie on the plate next to it. "Even if it's not true, you need to paint a picture for the court that you are stable. You, Levi Porter, cannot and will not be rocked. You are able to provide for Duncan like nobody ever can or will—"

"I can do that," I say, interjecting.

But Buzz isn't finished. "I need you to read between the lines," he murmurs, his elbows on his knees as he leans closer to me, as if taking me into his confidence. "It must *appear* that you're *settled down*. That you're in the process of making roots."

There's something in what he's saying that I'm starting to catch on to, not going to lie the extra emphasis he's placing on certain words helps. But would he really be advising me to try and put one over on the courts?

"Are you saying I should lie, because if—"

"No, I'm not saying that," Buzz snaps, holding up a hand and shaking his head. "There's nothing wrong with taking your truth and painting it a bit more, shall we say, abstract than what it really is. Kind of like the saying printed on a vehicle's side mirrors."

Now I'm really confused. From kids to cars in the blink of an eye. "Huh?"

"It says, 'Objects in mirror are closer than they appear.' In this case, it's that the objects may have a different relationship than what is really there." He looks me in the eye sternly, his expression so serious, I half-expect him to bust out a Power-Point presentation on the importance of eye contact in intense situations.

Somewhere in the recess of my brain, though, I'm starting to understand. A lightbulb goes off at the same moment a lightning bolt hits me in the side of my head. "You think I need to have a partner, a fiancée?"

Buzz sits back in his chair and shrugs his shoulders. "You said it, I didn't."

"Oh, come on." Throwing my hands in the air, I stand up. "I need to find someone to play house with me so I can be Duncan's guardian?"

"I'm not saying you have to, but I am saying it will help for you to appear to be headed in that direction."

There's a knock at the door, and the young intern appears, peeking his head through the doorway. "Sorry to interrupt. Mr. Sherman, you have your last appointment of the day in a few minutes."

"Ah." Buzz's eyebrows wiggle. "Thank you, Jim." As the door closes, Buzz hops up and looks at his hands. "I should get prepared for this. How are you feeling?"

How am I feeling? Horrible. Confused. Angry. Not enough.

"I guess I'll be okay. Once I find someone to marry me."

"That's the spirit." Buzz chuckles as the door opens again and a small woman carrying a bag of supplies enters, shooting a glance my way as she does. Seeing the look on my face, Buzz grins and holds up his hands. "Weekly manicure. I look at my hands a lot and I can't stand a hangnail. The bonus is the hand and palm massages. Amazing. My hands actually feel relaxed when we're done. Like wet, limp noodles ready for some sauce."

Only in Sweetkiss Creek.

Standing, I hold out my hand and shake his. "Thanks for your time, Buzz. I appreciate the advice."

"I assume you want me across this?"

"Please."

He nods to the papers on his desk. "I'll keep those here, then, and we'll do everything we can to make sure Duncan stays with you and your family. But in the meantime, get him more settled here and into a routine that's with you and the rest of the Porters. Something tangible where we can show that he's thriving under your care. You've got job stability, that's not a problem, but we want them to see you as a dad."

A few minutes later, after I've said goodbye and turned down the offer to get my nails done as well, I send a text to my mom so they know I'm okay. Then I point my car in the direction of a certain apartment building in town.

I could use a friend right now. My best friend.

I *need* to see Georgie.

EIGHT

Georgie

Locking the door of Pages and Prose, I grab the pile of empty boxes on the sidewalk beside me, carefully balancing everything so I can walk home. My apartment is only a few minutes away, which is awesome. I love the proximity; it was one of the reasons I'd chosen to rent that particular apartment. On the days I forget my lunch, I can run home and fix myself something. Plus, I get back each day to take Toto out at least once before I have to close the shop. I highly recommend living close to where you work to everyone.

When I opened my shop, I made sure it was on Magnolia Lane. It's the shopping area in Sweetkiss Creek, a little haven nestled down a lane in the middle of small-town Americana. If you're wondering where its name comes from, of course there are gorgeous magnolia trees lining the street. When they're all blooming, the area smells absolutely divine. It's the best.

My daily commute home includes a stroll past cafes, a florist, stores with boutique clothing and upscale children's items, bespoke jewelers who make one-of-a-kind baubles and other sparkly things for those who want one-of-a-kind things, and so much more. It's the perfect place for me. At least now it is. Even though my initial move here was supposed to be temporary, it seems that Sweetkiss Creek could be my forever home.

I shift the boxes from one side to the other in my arms and think about how the move here changed my perspective on life. Growing up the way I had wasn't easy, yet I'd done it. I made it to being an adult and mostly on my own. Actually, I take back the word "mostly"—I made it on my own. Period.

I skip up the porch steps of the old brick building that was once a three-story walk-up townhome, which had been converted ages ago, and in a matter of moments, I'm standing inside my apartment on the first floor. I painted it a bright white all throughout when I moved in because the walls were a weird dull yellow and kinda made me ill. The first time my friend Riley had come over and seen the white walls, she'd compared it to a hotel suite. She'd not meant it as a compliment, but I took it as one. I like that the walls are clean and fresh, because on the other hand, the furniture and my "things" are just a mess. Secondhand couch, the tiny dining room set someone gave me complete with a leg that likes to come off the table, and a TV that I found in the bookstore when I took over the lease.

I happened to win my mattress right after I moved here in a weird fluke, taking part in a social media contest when a local bedding store opened a town over in Lake Lorelei. It was a good thing I did because, for the first month I was here, I'd been sleeping on my floor on top of a pile of bedding. Bedding I'd purchased for a bed I'd get one day. So in a sense, I called that mattress to me. Like that movie *Field of Dreams*: build it and they will come.

Tossing the boxes to the side, I head to the back door and let Toto out before I look around and wonder where I should start first. I have seven days to evacuate. Where do I go? Worst case scenario, I guess I can set up camp in my bookshop, but storing my things is another matter.

I don't want to move again. I just don't want to. I love this place so much, but another part of me wonders that if I have to pack everything up, why not just break the lease or get out of it if I can get a new place?

A grunt from Toto, who has already come back inside and is flopping at my feet, reminds me why. Not many landlords get excited to hear that you have a giant Rottweiler as your roommate. I was lucky I was able to get a place on the first floor here. I'm pretty sure the sound of Toto walking back and forth on the second or even the third floor would be annoying for anyone who lives underneath us. I have needs, and special ones at that, with this dog.

"But you're mine," I whisper, kissing the top of his head. Dark black eyes search mine, darting toward the boxes. He knows something's up. Doggie intuition. It's a thing.

I take a box and toss it over by my bookshelf, a find from a local yard sale, and grab the remote, finding a playlist on Spotify. The sounds of Coldplay soothe me as I start pulling titles from the shelf and get to work, determined to fill these boxes before I start dinner.

Just as I grab the first few books there's a knock at my door, which causes Toto to race over and stand quietly behind it. I love that he doesn't bark if someone knocks; he just waits like a good, silent, stoic soldier to see if he needs to pounce. One word from me and he will. I just have to say "gotcha" and he'll chase you. If I want him to stop, it's a simple "here here" and he'll come back. There's also "friends" which I use so he knows any other person who is with us is good and he doesn't need to be on guard. Somehow we'd managed to come up with these signals together and they work. Luckily I've only had to use "gotcha" once. It was still one time too many.

When I look through the peephole, a flutter ripples

through my chest. Levi is standing outside my front door and it totally surprises me. My hands fly up to my hair, which feels like a matted mess. I pull it out of the high ponytail I'd looped it in and give it a shake, only to second-guess myself. It feels desperate, so instead I whip it all into a bun at the base of my neck instead.

As I open the door, I motion for Toto to stand down, which he does by planting himself beside me and watching the door. There's a grin making its way across my face and I don't want to stop it.

"Hey." I fling the door open so Levi can come inside. "What brings you to these parts?"

"Can't get enough of you," he says with a chuckle, causing a liftoff of heat in the area surrounding my heart. If only.

"Don't you know how to make a girl feel special." I wave my hand for him to come inside. "Just got home myself."

Levi struts in, walking over to Toto and patting his head. Toto is still tense, unmoving but keeping his eyes on Levi. He knows Levi and trusts him, but I've trained him to stay on alert. We've trusted before and been burned.

"Friends," I remind him, patting Levi's arm.

Levi's eyes widen as Toto visibly relaxes, his whole Rottie demeanor changing as soon as I say the word. "It's amazing to me that you have your own language with that dog."

"I should have trained him in German," I say with a wink. "Then you'd be really impressed."

"The fact that you have like, four or five words that only the two of you know and he'll listen to them is impressive." Levi scans my living room, his eyes landing on the boxes immediately. "What's going on there?"

"I have to move out temporarily." Sighing, I fling myself into a wingback chair. "There's termites in this building, and they've done a number on the foundation. Apparently, there are stability issues they need to sort out, but I've got to leave. Seven days to evacuate."

"Is that legal?"

I nod. "It is. There's a lawyer a few doors down from the bookshop, Elaine Lenhart. I went to see her this afternoon to make sure, and she said that my landlord is within their legal right to do it, but they do have to reimburse me for at least four days of being ousted from my home."

"So they'll pay for a hotel? And your food?"

I shrug. "To some degree. There's compensation, but it's all so vague I'm not sure what's going to be compensated exactly. The rental company said they'll do everything they can to make it so it doesn't feel like we're gone very long, but that makes me laugh." I stretch my arms over my head, loosening my knotted shoulders and fighting a yawn. "It's not like I'm in a position to just take a day off work and move everything, nor am I some kind of witch who can wiggle her nose and everything's boxed up and moved into storage, you know? I have to put it all away, then get it all somewhere plus find a place to live. In seven days. While running a business."

I bang my head against the back of my chair, a favorite of mine even if it is close to falling apart, thanking my lucky stars for its softness. It's a good chair, it's just old. Rolling my head to the side, I look at Levi. "Sorry. I'm just irritated."

"Look, friends help each other, right? I've got time on my hands, I can help you." His tone is so sincere as he reaches out and puts a hand on my knee. I can't help but let my gaze fall to where his skin touches mine, a warmth I could get used to. He leans closer to where I sit, and squeezes. "What do you need to do? Where can we start?"

"Really?"

"Really."

Nodding my head to the corner of the room behind him, I

indicate to the pile of boxes. "I want to fill those tonight. It'll make me feel a lot better if I do."

"Done. Won't take us long either, so we can go and get more boxes tonight if you want. I know a storage place on the outskirts of town that sells cardboard boxes for moving. While we're there, we can see about rental fees."

I'm pretty sure my shoulders are sliding down back to their original position just under my ears now. He makes it sound so...easy. "Yes, please."

Levi jumps up and holds out his hand. I look at it for a moment, the warmth of his gesture sinking in, before I slide my hand into his and let him pull me to my feet. It's a simple gesture, but in that moment, I feel a flutter in my chest, a realization dawning on me that maybe, just maybe, there's something more between us than I've been willing to admit.

Once I'm up and we're facing each other, neither one of us lets go. We're suspended in time for a brief moment, as if something is shifting between us in this lightning bolt of a second.

One of his fingers traces a circle on the inside of my palm as the other fingers squeeze my hand gently, this simple act setting off a flash of heat underneath my skin. My thumb, in return, moves slowly back and forth across the back of his hand as we stare at one another. There's a sensation of electricity, a current of fire that rages through me in an instant.

My heart races, I'm sure he can hear it slamming inside of me. My breath hitches as my eyes land on his lips. Big, full, beautiful smooth red lips that I've often wondered about kissing. Thoughts I've learned to shove to the side because I value his friendship. So much.

But as I drag my eyes slowly back to his, I'm pretty sure I catch him looking at my lips, too. The movement is so quick and fluid, I'm not sure if I did, but my body is reacting as if he was.

This is it. The thing you hear about.

This must be what it means to have your breath taken away.

A moment like this needs to be acknowledged or it never happened. Right? I want to pull my eyes from his, but I can't. They are the most perfect blue, not a sky blue but with more depth, like the Hope Diamond. I saw it on display once, years ago, at the Smithsonian in Washington D.C. but it obviously made an impression.

Right now, however, my attention is on this man who stands in front of me. There's delight dancing behind those bright blue eyes, laughter lingers, and there's a promise of more. I can feel it even if it is fleeting.

Closing my eyes, I calm myself, wanting to say something. I do my breathwork, breathing in and out slowly, counting to five each time. Only, there is a smell that hits my senses. Like... rotten eggs?

Oh, for the love of all things Taylor Swift, there is an odor floating around us that could knock out a wooden puppet, and that can only mean one thing.

"Oh my..." Levi chokes. "What is that?"

"Toto," I say, pulling my hand away from the comfort of his so I can fan my face. "And his almighty butt. That is the smell of a dog who has farted."

"New plan," he suggests. "How about we take him for a walk and get a bite to eat? I know where the best barbeque in all of North Carolina is. Then we come back and pack?"

Giggling, I cover my mouth and nose with one hand as I swipe Toto's leash from its hook by the front door with the other. "Last one to make it outside alive buys dinner."

When he said he knew where the best barbeque was in all of North Carolina, that man was not lying. Pulled pork barbeque sandwiches are my favorite, and the one I'm enjoying now has knocked my socks off.

My mouth waters as I lift the sandwich to my mouth, take another bite, and groan loudly as I do, causing the man sitting beside me on the park bench to laugh.

"I told you these were the best," Levi says between bites. "This place has been around since my mom was a little girl."

"I love the history here," I say after I swallow another mouthful. "It makes it even more special to live somewhere that has such a rich and vibrant past." I hold my sandwich in the air and grin. "I get to see through your lens some days, too, which makes it even more special."

A flush hits Levi's cheeks. "You see it through my lens?"

"I sure do." I wave my hand at the park around us. "In the past year that I've known you, you've shown me a lot of what this place has to offer. I knew what Sweetkiss Creek had going for it, but going on hikes with you through the mountains, trying whitewater rafting and inner tubing…I've even camped solo one night all because you encouraged me to give it a try."

Levi points to Toto. "You also have a massive guard dog to take with you when you camp out."

"That is true." I laugh. "But I'm out of my comfort zone, you know? That's what I wanted to do and why I left New York City when I did."

Levi chews thoughtfully, turning in his seat on the bench to face me. "You've only told me that you left New York because you wanted something better, but you've never elaborated."

I nod. "No, I guess I haven't."

"Care to…elaborate?"

Putting my sandwich back in its wrapper, I look at the

ground, summoning my words. This is one story I've not shared with anyone here since I moved to Sweetkiss Creek. It's my backstory and not one I'm proud of, but it's mine.

Actually, I take that back. I am proud of it because I'm the one who came through it all, but still. Levi Porter is about to get a whole lot of me being really vulnerable and raw.

"I think we're in a place where I can do that." I say my words slowly, giving myself time to summon my courage.

"Hit me with it," Levi says with a laugh, nudging me in my ribs with his elbow. "What was childhood and family life like for you in New York?"

"To start with, I didn't have one." I let my gaze meet his, his eyebrows furrowing.

"You didn't have a family? Or a childhood?"

"I've never met my parents, Levi," I say softly. "At least, not my real ones. I was put into the foster system when I was little because they couldn't take care of themselves. I'm one of those kids who bounced around from foster home to foster home, hoping and praying I'd be adopted but wasn't."

Silence slams between us like a door hit by a strong wind. I can tell by the look on his face that he's horrified he even brought it up now, so I reach out and pat his arm.

"It's fine, now. I'm here and I took care of myself to get here."

His lips, smiling a moment ago, are now taut. "But it couldn't have been easy."

"It wasn't. I got a job as soon as I could make money. I worked fast food, mowing lawns, cleaning houses...whatever I needed to do, and I saved every penny."

"As a teenager?"

I nod. "Yep. I worked around studying because I knew I wanted to graduate high school and get a diploma. I wasn't happy. I was in homes where there was always a circumstance;

one family was only fostering so they could collect the checks, and another had a super sweet mother but the father had a temper—that house I ran away from, which didn't go over well. The third one I was placed in, one of the other kids bullied the rest of us and I ended up getting into a fight with him."

"What?"

"He tried to steal one of the younger kids' lunches one day when we were waiting for the school bus. So, I...hit him." I hold up my right hand, balling it into a fist. "Tiny but mighty. I knocked out one of his front teeth."

Levi nearly spits out his sandwich. "Sorry. I'm trying to deal with this visual of you punching some guy. Good on you; someone needed to defend the younger kids."

"Someone had to do it, but I hate fighting. I hate anger and yelling." Of course, it comes from all of the different houses I lived in. One hundred percent. It was like being on a game show and not knowing which prize you'd get when you spun the wheel.

"Of course you do, I'm not saying you're condoning it," Levi murmurs, inching closer to me. "How come you've not told me about this before?"

"I don't tell anyone this, Levi. I'm trying to make new memories that I can hold on to that are happy ones. That's why the bookstore is so special to me."

"So you saved enough money as a teen to open it?"

"Kind of, but not really." I chuckle. "I was able to open the store with a grant for underprivileged women. There was a businesswoman out of Charlotte who ran a competition years ago asking for business proposals from single women who needed help. I was lucky enough to make it to the final, and win support. I used that money to rent the space and order my first few boxes of books. From there, the rest has worked out because I've worked hard on it."

There's something different in his eyes, watching me as he listens. "I had no idea."

"It's not like I advertise it." I take my last bite of this amazing pork sandwich and chew, staring at the park grounds. I shiver uncontrollably as the sun begins to dip behind the trees, a movement that doesn't go unnoticed by Levi.

"Here," he says as he shrugs out of his zip-up hoodie, putting it over my shoulders. "You're cold."

"Thank you," I say, pulling it tightly around me. It's fleeting, but I catch a whiff of Levi's cologne—a hint of bergamot and sandalwood mixed together. My senses are in overdrive; he's like a comfortable blanket holding me safe. "I've worked hard for what I have, which is why I think I'm freaking out that I need to evacuate my apartment right now. I don't like being told I *have* to go."

"I get it, and thank you." Levi's hand is suddenly on top of mine, squeezing it. "Thank you for trusting me enough to share that with me."

I don't dare look down, even though I want to. I just want to enjoy this moment with Levi sitting here comforting me while we eat our food. I want to burn the feeling he gives me into my memory banks so I can return to it later, when I'm alone at home and wishing I was brave enough to speak up and tell him how I feel.

I'll also try to tell myself that I'm not really falling for him and haven't been all this time because that's a fun game I play in my head, but at least it's safe. Because he's another part of me I don't want to ever go away, especially not now that I have him in my universe.

"You know," he says, interrupting my internal spiral, "Austin and I were in town checking on some of our rental properties this morning. One of them is not far from the bookstore and it's empty right now. I've been thinking of fixing it up for Duncan and me to move into, but maybe you could stay there while they work on your place?"

"Are you serious?" Who is this guy? Prince Charming? "Oh my gosh, Levi, yes! If you're serious, that would help me so much."

"Of course I'm serious." Despite the happiness in my voice and the sincerity in his question, his face is dark and he keeps his eyes on the ground, pulling his hand off of mine. I miss his warmth as soon as it's gone.

Throwing my hands around his neck, I pull him tight. "You're my hero. Thank you!" I sit back and chuckle. "That was too easy, but it's you. You're like a godsend."

He shrugs. "It's nothing."

"Stop that." I put my hand on his shoulder. "If there's anything I can do in return for you, you have to let me know. I appreciate where your heart is, but now that you've heard my background, you have to understand I know that there's never a free ride."

Levi goes quiet, nodding his head slowly, his eyes scanning the park. I can tell he's thinking. I wait quietly, wondering if he's already regretting offering me the apartment to use, when he clears his throat and pulls his shoulders back.

"Since you mentioned it," he begins, his energy suddenly vibing quite anxious, "there's something I want to ask you for in return."

"A little *quid pro quo*, Clarice?" I tease, quoting from one of our favorite scary movies, *Silence of the Lambs*, but he's still not smiling. "Levi, I just revealed my sad, sad backstory to you. You can tell me anything. You can ask me anything, we're friends. We're good friends—in fact, I think it's fair to say we're more than that. You've been one of the best friends a girl could ever ask for. You literally just offered me a place to live... how can I *help* you?"

He struggles with his words, his lips twisting and turning

as if he's trying to find the right thing to say. I don't like that he's suddenly so stressed, so I go back to silence and give him a little space. As I settle in on the bench again, his phone dings, pulling his attention to a text he's suddenly focused on, so I stand up and stretch while he holds up a finger asking me to wait a minute.

"Sorry. It's Mom, asking me about Duncan." He nods to the phone in his hand. "I need to call her quickly."

"I can wait," I say as I pull out my phone. "I can keep myself busy with my own device, thank you very much."

Levi hops up and disappears around a tree, talking in a hushed tone to his mother. I feel like there's a small case of Dr. Jekyll and Mr. Hyde happening here, where he's gone from being super chill and relaxed to uptight and stressed, and it's happened in a matter of moments. Seeing as his whole world has flip-flopped in the past few months, I'm sure the responsibility of having Duncan and stepping up to kind of be a dad can do that to a person.

As I flip through emails and my social media feed, I let my hand fall to my side to pat the top of Toto's head. My man. My main guy. The one who will not leave my side. Everyone needs a Toto.

I let my eyes wander over to where Levi paces under a giant magnolia, the scent of its flowers wafting around me. I love them so much. Such a delicate white flower perched on a staunch tree. The fragile blooms supported by the strength underneath.

Levi's shoulders hunch slightly and he keeps casting his eyes my way, making me wonder if the call is about me. Have I done something wrong? My own anxiety kicks in, and I question the offer for the apartment now. Maybe his mom had plans for it and he's telling her that he's letting me use it and now she's upset?

He disconnects the call and slides the phone into his back

pocket. The sun is all but gone from the sky; it's getting dark now and I can make out the first firefly sightings of the night as bright lights twinkle off and on again in a slow cadence in the trees around us.

It's actually quite romantic here, a thought I work to push to the back of my brain as Levi appears back in front of me.

"Everything okay?"

"Huh?" he asks.

"Levi!" This distracted version of Levi is so not him. Still gripping my phone in one hand, I stare at him. "At home. You said your mom texted you and you had to call about Duncan. Is he okay, is everything okay at home?"

"Oh, yes," he answers me, visibly flustered. "Sorry. He's fine. She's fine. We're all fine."

There is nothing fine about that sentence. "Okay, now you sound really weird."

"Sorry," he apologizes once more as he begins again. "Where was I, you know, before Mom wanted me to call?"

"You had something to ask me. A favor in return for staying at your apartment." I jump to my feet and put a hand on each of his arms, studying him as much as myself. "And look, if having use of the apartment is too much right now or if me needing help is too overwhelming, I get it. Just tell me it's a no-go and I'll go back to finding a motel where Toto and I can hole up for a couple weeks."

"No, no. It's not that…" Levi shoves both of his hands in the front pockets of his jeans and stares at the ground. I can feel my heartbeat in my eardrums, it's that intense.

"Levi," I begin, "you're kind of freaking me out here. What's going on?"

He smiles, he frowns. He looks up, he looks down. Through it all, he stays in front of me, allowing me to help brace him. It's not much, but I feel like maybe my touch is helping, but I can't tell. He won't look at me. He's dropped his gaze to the ground, staring at our feet now.

What. Happened?

After what feels like an eternity, he slowly drags his gaze upward to meet mine.

"How would you feel about...getting engaged?"

NINE

Levi

Well, that escalated quickly.

It sounded good in my head, but in retrospect, I should have taken a moment to think about what I was actually saying with my mouth and how it was coming across before I opened that big hole in my face.

As soon as the words painfully tumbled out, I watched in super slow motion as Georgie lost her grip on the iPhone in her hands. It does a somersault in the air, sticking its landing with a crack, the pointy corner of the phone and its case managing to connect with her foot.

There's a pause of stunned realization before she lets out a yelp that rivals a howler monkey, hopping around on one foot while clutching the other. It's like watching a slapstick comedy unfold before my eyes, complete with exaggerated expressions of pain and a dramatic reenactment of the entire event.

"OW!" Georgie shrieks, folding on top of herself as she hits the ground, falling to her butt and staring at her foot. "What did I just do?"

I kneel beside her swiftly, sliding her Converse off and checking the top of her foot out. There's a spot that's red and a small welt rising to the surface. Who would have thought an iPhone of all things could do such damage and so quickly?

"You've smacked it really good right around your metatarsals," I say pointing to the place on her foot just below her toes where all of the tiniest bones in our body hang out. The poor girl writhes in pain, opening her mouth to do a silent scream. "There's nerve endings there, too. Probably why the pain is reverberating so much."

"Ohhh," she groans, sitting back and using her hands to brace herself as she shakes her head and laughs. "So ridiculous."

"Can you stand?"

"Of course." She gives me a sheepish look. "It was only a phone."

Still, I hold out my hand, overjoyed when her hand slides into mine. I know she's in pain, but I still have to work hard to keep my eyes from staring at her lips. I never realized how pink they were until today, and I know she caught me staring at them.

I get up first and brace myself, letting her put her full weight on me. She stands and holds onto me tightly for a few minutes—not that I'm going to ask her to go away—before she puts her foot down and walks in a circle around me. It's slow, but she is moving.

"It's sore," she says, surprised. "Like, it feels weird and it hurts."

"Probably will be for a day or two, but you should be good after."

She stops moving long enough to give me a little side-eye. "You know, I could have sworn you just kind of proposed to me."

"Yeah," I begin, "about that..."

I fill her in on my movements over the past few hours: from the papers being served to my visit with the lawyer. She nods her head as I speak, listening intently, her eyes growing wider and wider as I mention the part about how it would be good for me if I looked more settled.

"So, let me get this straight," she says, tucking a strand of honey-blond hair behind one ear. "You want me to be your fake fiancée?"

"Yes," I say with a groan, "but in exchange, you've got the apartment."

"I'm sure I could have the apartment anyway," she says, narrowing her eyes.

She scares me a little when she gets like this. I kinda like it. "I debated asking, but when you said to ask if you could do anything in return, well...I was hoping for some help here and I guess it seemed like it would be more believable if it was you I was engaged to."

I'm making a mess of this. Worst proposal ever, not that it really is one. Even if I wanted it to be one, I'm making mental notes to myself as to what NOT to do in the future.

In my head, I'm on an amusement park ride. It's not quite a roller coaster, more like being stuck on a loop inside "It's a Small World" where I keep seeing the same thing and hearing the same song over and over. And she won't stop laughing now.

"Wow, if this was really you asking me to marry you, I'd be so disappointed." She looks around us, scanning the area. "Is there a secret camera nearby?"

"No," I say, grabbing her hands and pulling her toward me. Anything I can do to touch her, it seems. "Just your good friend asking you for one really crazy favor."

Georgie's gaze finds mine, dark green flecks appearing in light brown eyes as they sparkle. They rock back and forth, searching, before she sighs. "Fine. I'll do it."

Be still my heart. "Really?"

"Yes." She stands back from me and smiles. "I want to do

it, and not just because you're letting me use the apartment. I want to help you and Duncan. That boy deserves to be surrounded by a good family and the Porters are a good family."

A warmth fills my heart. "Thanks. You know, we consider you part of that family, too."

An odd expression flashes across her face, but it's so fleeting I almost think I'm imagining things. In the next instant, Georgie is all smiles, sunshine, and cupcakes.

"That's sweet of you to say." She shoves her hands in her pockets and, using her chin, indicates toward the park exit. "Maybe we should get back to my place and fill a box or two? I wouldn't want you to be too late getting home to the little guy."

"Sure," I say, a tiny feeling of my own guilt panging inside me. I'm just not sure if it's for Duncan or what I've asked of my best friend. I watch as she takes a few steps in front of me, appearing to be solid for a stride or two before limping.

"Hey," I say, standing in front of her with my back to her. "Jump up. I'll give you a piggyback ride."

"Seriously?" She laughs. "What about Toto?"

"I can hold his leash, too, but you're limping. The more rest you can get right now, the better. Trust me." I hold up my right hand, the reminder of an old injury I've dealt with for the last few years, the result of an on-field incident. "Been there."

"It was a phone, Levi, it's not like I was playing football. I'll shake it off."

"I've seen weirder injuries from smaller items, trust me." I stay put and hold my hands out to the side. "Jump on, c'mon."

I hear a huff right before I feel her hands as she places them on my shoulders.

"You just want to be engaged so you have an excuse to boss me around."

Now there's an idea. "Will it work?"

"Probably not." She jumps up, and I catch her easily, my hands gripping around each leg and holding her close. Her scent hits me: coconut and lime. My favorite. I wonder if my mom can turn that scent into an ice cream flavor? I'll have to ask.

Georgie's heels dig into my sides. "Giddyup, now, I've got things to do. Let's go."

Grinning from ear to ear, I squeeze her legs, making her buck and giggle. Just the sound of her laugh sends a huge thrill through my system.

I could get used to this.

***

"You're going to do what now?"

Everyone, and by everyone I mean my mom and Austin, stands stock still, frozen in place. I'd walked in the door a few minutes ago and found them sitting here. Mom's newest habit is to sit down after dinner and work on a puzzle, while Austin likes to hover and help.

"I'm going to be engaged. I guess I'm engaged." I stop and think about it for a moment. Am I officially faux engaged now? Or do I need to make an announcement so we can consider it a for-real fake engagement? "I'd better check with Georgie because I think we are."

"You *think* you're engaged?" Austin manages to say loudly between laughs.

"Hey, keep it down." Aware that his voice carries and not sure where in the house Duncan is lurking, I put a finger to my lips. "Can we ixnay on the engaged-ay?"

"You said it," he retorts defensively, as only a brother can.

"I whispered it." I know I'm hissing, but the sound of something being dropped on the floor above us proves my point. I stare at the ceiling. "I don't want everyone to know yet."

My brother isn't getting the memo. "But you're getting fake married. I say we tell everyone!" He barks more laughter, holding his sides. "Does this mean I need to get you a fake wedding gift? If so, I'm springing for the fake honeymoon. My treat. You can pick Atlantis for all I care—it's fake."

I'm about to read my brother the Riot Act when Duncan appears in the doorway in his pajamas.

"Hey bud," I say walking over to greet him. "Are we being too loud?"

He shakes his head, his eyes scanning the room, falling on each one of us individually as he looks around. He takes a big breath and then turns to face me and only me.

"Were you with Georgie?"

I nod. "Sure was. She needed help so I went to see what I could do." I ruffle his hair, grateful for the exchange. "Why? Everything okay?"

"Do you think she'll let me work at the store again?" His eyes dart around, checking out our audience, but thankfully both Mom and Austin are pretending like nothing is happening. Nothing just south of extraordinary, that is. He is *talking* to me. Conversing. Conversating. Chitchat, paddy whack.

"I'm sure she'd love it if you were to come back. How about if we call her tomorrow and you can ask her yourself?"

Duncan bites his lower lip, thinking about what I've said, and slowly begins to nod his head. "Okay. Let's do that, but I don't want to get paid. I want to work for books."

I sneak a sideways glance at my mother, who's grinning from ear to ear. As a book lover herself, I know this is music to her ears.

"Tell you what, as soon as we're done with breakfast tomorrow morning, we'll call her. Sound good?"

"Yes," he says in a serious tone, but with a very teeny, tiny smile on his lips.

I honestly can't believe we're having this much of an exchange. I'll take it. As much as he wants to give, I'll take it. But I also need to know what the connection is.

"So, you like her, huh?" When Duncan tilts his head to the side, I expound. "Georgie. You two seem to get along."

He nods, pushing his bangs off his forehead, and shrugs. "I guess. She's different. She didn't treat me weird when I stole from her. She's like, giving me a chance. You know?"

"I do know," I respond, "and I'm glad that the two of you can talk. She's special, isn't she?"

Duncan lets his gaze flit around the room once more as he nods in agreement. He opens his mouth like he's going to say more but then snaps it closed. I'd have to be a dolt to not see the exhaustion that washes over him suddenly. "You know what, I'm tired."

"I bet you are. There's been a lot going on the last few weeks." I wait for him to walk away, but it's Duncan's turn to surprise me once more as he leans forward and wraps his arms around my middle, squeezing me tight.

"Good night, Levi."

He races down the hallway, leaving me listening as he trots upstairs. I wait for the slam of his bedroom door. When all of these bedtime steps of his new nightly routine have been completed, I let out a breath of air and turn to find my mother and brother watching me with smug satisfaction.

"What?"

"He's settling in," Austin says as he gets up from his spot on the couch. He shakes his empty glass in the air. "Anybody want anything from the kitchen?"

"Hot tea for me," Mom replies, keeping her eyes trained

on me. She waits for Austin to leave the room before she pounces.

"That boy," she says, wagging a finger in the air, "is very impressionable right now."

"It's about him, but it also isn't." I pull a chair closer to where she sits on the couch. "I don't want to hurt him because of my choices, but this is one time when a choice is made in order to help."

"We can keep the secret and protect him from the adult drama of it all, we just have to all be on the same page." She looks at the puzzle pieces laid out on the coffee table in front of her, snatching one up and clicking it into place like she knew it was there the whole time. "I'm also worried about Georgie."

"She's fine; we talked and she's okay to do this." I sit back, rubbing my hands on my knees.

"Are you sure this is a good idea?"

"For Duncan? Yes, I do. I want to present the best possible case so I can keep him." I feel tears springing to my eyes. Who knew I would feel this pent-up about this kid, but I am starting to really care about him. Plus, Tom wanted me to do this. Me and only me.

"I'm not talking about Duncan," she murmurs, hazel eyes rising to meet mine. "I'm talking about Georgie."

"What do you mean?"

"What I mean is, are you sure it's a good idea for you to pretend to be engaged to the woman you're secretly in love with?"

TEN

Georgie

I've never moved into an apartment unseen. But because I'm now on crutches, it's the way things are going. First time for everything, right?

When I dropped my phone two days ago and it hit my foot, I'd gone to bed that night with it kind of hurting only to wake up around two in the morning with a searing pain shooting up my leg. It was the kind of intense pain that happens if you break something, only I knew I hadn't broken anything...or at least I thought I hadn't.

I made it through a very sleepless night and dragged myself to the local doctor the next morning. After an hour of examining me, taking a scan, and doing some reflex work, he could only figure that I'd managed to hit a nerve and irritate it, inflaming it. I was prescribed a few days on crutches, some aspirin, and rest. It's not even a cool injury, like I can't tell anyone I did it skateboarding. "I was trying to perfect my Crooked Grind, when all of a sudden..." No.

This is evidenced when Austin sees me as he arrives at my apartment building to pick me up and the first boxes of my things to go to the new place.

"Okay, how did this happen again?" He shakes his head incredulously. "I mean, Levi told me, but I really want to hear it from you."

Oh, these Porter boys and their humor. They should take it on the road.

"Save it for your podcast," I grumble, tilting my head to the side.

"It's on summer hiatus," he says with a wink. He points at my foot. "Did your phone really do that?"

"I know, it's nuts, but yes." I half laugh, half cringe as I sit on the porch holding Toto's leash, watching Austin load boxes. "It's pretty embarrassing."

"Good timing, too. Not like you had to move this week or anything," he says as he tosses the last box into the bed of his pickup truck and reaches for one of the three suitcases I've got packed. "You know, you don't have much out here for a woman who's moving into a new space today."

"It's only temporary. The rest of my things are being picked up by a moving company later today and taken to a storage unit." Not that they need to be saved; I mean, the bed maybe, but the rest of it is due to be replaced. But since my rental company did finally pony up and say they'd pay for storage and reimburse me up to two thousand dollars for the inconvenience, I decided to take the storage unit.

Austin picks up the last piece of luggage and closes the back of his truck.

"You and your brother are being really nice to offer me this place," I call out from my perch.

Austin turns and looks at me, cocking his head to one side. "Well, considering you're marrying him—"

"Let's not get crazy." I cackle, nervousness teetering in my laugh as Levi's SUV appears on the street. He slows and blocks the road as he flicks on his hazards and jumps out. Mary, his mother, is right behind him. Is it wrong of me that I hope she brought some ice cream?

"Hey," he says easily, his smile fading as he sees the state I'm in. "Oh, wow, you're really hurt, aren't you?"

"Did you think I was making it up?" I tease back. Holding out my crutches, I hop around in a circle, slowly, like a super-model showing off the latest in bespoke crutch-wear. "It's very sporty, but also sleek with the right pair of shoes."

"This is exactly why cell phones are dangerous," Mary says as she wags a finger in the air. She comes over and gives me a hug.

"Tell me about it. I'm rethinking having my landline put back in." I eye the older woman suspiciously. "What are you doing here?"

"I had to come by and say hello, considering you're now engaged to my son."

My eyes slam into Levi's and he cuts his to the side, avoiding me. I look back over her way and force a tiny smile. "Yes. Well, I see the cat is out of the fake bag."

Mary holds a hand up in the air, cutting me off. "I don't want to be privy to any other info other than what I know now. Best to not tell me anything."

"We get why you guys are doing it, but Mom doesn't want to be guilty by association." Austin laughs as he hops behind the wheel of the truck. Luckily, the windows are rolled down because he realizes he forgot something. "Hey, is Toto coming with me?"

"Yes, please," I say, handing the leash off to Levi who leads him to the pickup truck. The plan being for me to ride with Levi, and Mary, too, I guess, over to the new place. "Thanks again."

Austin eyes my baby as he walks toward the truck, drooling. Toto can't help it, it's a Rottie thing and I love it.

"Don't be scared, Austin," I call out playfully. "He's only

injured one man in my life and that's because he was making fun of me."

Austin grimaces as Levi opens the passenger-side door and helps hoist my big old, dragon-like dog into the seat next to Austin. "You look good with a dog in that truck, Austin. They're a lady magnet, you know."

Austin and Toto give each other side-eyes. "If this dog is a lady magnet, I'm the governor of North Carolina."

We watch in silence as the odd couple pulls away and makes their way down the street. My eyes flick from Levi to his mother and back to the SUV. I really want to be in that car right now, in the backseat, without her inquiring eyes watching me. I feel very judged right now for my decision and part in this whole situation.

It's temporary, Georgie. It's a fake engagement for a friend and we'll go back to normal...right?

As if he's read my mind, Levi reaches out and takes the crutches from me, handing them to his mom. "Come on, let's get you moved in."

Laughing, I watch as my walking utensils disappear with Mary into the SUV. "How am I supposed to get in the car now?"

In one swoop, Levi wraps his arms around my waist and cradles me close to his chest, carrying me down the sidewalk to the SUV. I can feel his strength when he does, biceps flexing under his soft cotton T-shirt.

And it's also quite nice to be pressed up against his chest.

Startled, I go to wrap my arms around his neck to hold on, but find my hands stopping as they graze one of his biceps instead. I can't help it, I am such a bicep girl. I palm his bicep and then, the audacity, I keep it there for a second or two more just because of the thrill it sends into my system.

What is it about the flex and bulge of a man's muscle that

can make a woman quiver deep inside in a way she simply can't control?

"Like what you feel?" Levi growls in my ear as he approaches the vehicle. Snapping to look his way, I find him chewing back a grin.

"Can't argue," I manage to say, my voice a touch shaky. "It's a nice, ah, muscle you've got there, friend."

Friend? What am I even saying? I mean, I can say my voice is shaky because I'm obviously injured, but these words of mine are like a salad of ridiculousness.

Levi shakes his head and has no time to respond because the back door of the SUV opens. When I glance over, my smile grows wider when I see Duncan waiting there and waving.

"Hey, buddy," I coo as Levi places me on the seat beside him.

Mary turns in her seat to face us.

"Look," Duncan says, placing a stack of old comic books in my lap. "Do you see these? I found them this morning when we stopped at the gas station. Comic books. At a gas station! How cool!"

I stare at the comic books. Archie and Friends. "You've got great taste, Duncan. These were my favorites when I was a little girl."

"Really?" He grins at me as he tosses a Betty and Veronica comic book in my lap. "I got this one, too."

"For me?"

He nods, and as he does, I notice the cookbook is on the floor at his feet.

"Are you studying up on how to make me dinner, too?"

Duncan giggles. "I thought you may like to borrow it while you get settled. I'll want it back, though."

"Of course you will, but I thought it was a present?" I flick my eyes toward Mary in the front seat.

Duncan shrugs. "I decided I need to do something else for

her." He looks at the cookbook. "I wanted it because my mom loved Jamie Oliver."

I pick up the cookbook and place it in my lap. "Then I will take very good care of this and make sure to give it back to you as soon as I'm done with it. Or maybe we'll make something for dinner together one night. What do you say?"

"Cool," Duncan says, done now and turning to look out the window.

Up in the front seat, I've noticed two heads moving and turning. Mary's movements seem stunted, as if she's in shock at the conversation she's bearing witness to.

"Will you have Netflix at your place?" Duncan asks, turning his attention back to me.

"Probably," I say with a shrug. "If not today, soon. Why? Do you want to watch something on Netflix?"

"Riverdale. Duh." He winks at me. "It's Archie's show, you know."

Laughing, I throw my arm around my new little best friend. "We'll talk to Levi and see what he thinks about you watching it, okay?"

The car slows outside my new building, which I know is mine only because of the photos Levi sent me yesterday so it wouldn't fully be a "sight unseen" situation. The building is fairly new with retail spaces on the first floor and apartments above, all except one—a three-bedroom unit that takes up both floors. It boasts a fenced-in backyard, much larger than the one I have at my place and perfect for Toto, plus a large balcony stretching across two bedrooms in the back.

Levi opens the door and helps me out, Mary handing me my crutches as he jogs over to help Austin. The Porter brothers race in and out of the building, taking my things inside with Duncan helping as Mary and I make our way up the steps.

We're at the base of them when she stops me, placing a hand on my arm.

"Okay, I know I said I didn't want to know any more info, but I have to ask"—her eyes flick toward the building, making sure the boys are not within earshot—"if you really are okay with this fake engagement thing?"

When my eyes meet hers, I see a mother's worry. Not that I have much experience with it, considering my background, but I have my intuition around what it would be like. Mary's always been nice to me, but I know she's protective and loves her sons with all of her heart. I can only imagine that she must be worried for Levi and now Duncan, too.

"It's *quid pro quo*, isn't it?" I say as I hand her my crutches again and balance myself, holding the rail so I can hobble up the steps. "I needed a place to stay and Levi needs to look like he's settling down."

Emerald-green flecks appear in hazel eyes that flash with curiosity. It's as if this woman has a way of seeing into my soul. "Is it playing house for you?"

Oooff. Talk about being put on the spot. "It's about making sure Duncan ends up with the right person to raise him."

"And it's also about getting a free place to crash, right?"

Turning my head to the front door, I look up and find Levi at the top of the steps, one hand on his hip as he stares at his mother. "I told you, please don't insert yourself into this, Mom. I know you're not a fan of this plan, but it's what I'm choosing to do."

"You inserted me the day you told me," she says, trudging up the steps, shaking a finger at him. "So you shush and don't tell your mother how to feel."

"It's only temporary," I call out, hoping to make it all sound better than it must. "Once the case is settled, Levi and I can quietly call things off."

She watches us both. "I'm not trying to poke holes or make you change your minds, I just want to make sure you both know what can happen here. Plus," she says as she looks at me, "it is now quite clear to me that you, out of all of us, have a very special kinship with that child. We all need to be very, very careful."

As she disappears inside the building, Levi and I share a look. He lifts both shoulders, letting them drop. "It's not that she's mad, she's worried."

"I know." And I do, but I also can't take the gravity of all of this right now. I forgot to put on deodorant and I'm starting to feel ripe. Gripping the metal banister leading to the front door, I place all my weight down and start to do my lift and hobble move, but Levi is back at my side, coming to my rescue again.

"Stop that," he says, his tone filled with gravel and heat. "Let me."

For the second time this morning, he scoops me up like a sack of feathers and carries me over the threshold. Literally.

The front door opens, and my heart drops. This is the most beautiful open space I've ever seen. High ceilings, lots of light...a blank canvas needing some serious interior design love.

"It's even more stunning than the photos made it seem," I breathe out.

The few boxes I brought with me are stacked in the center of the living room, which Levi somehow had time to furnish in the last forty-eight hours. He points to the overstuffed L-shaped sofa. "You're to rest there; I'll go grab Toto."

I park myself on the couch, smelling its newness. "Did this just come out of the factory?"

Levi chuckles. "No idea, but it did just arrive this morning from Mr. Altman's store."

"We should get going," Mary announces, looking pointedly at Duncan. "Are you ready, boss?"

He nods, keeping his eyes on me as he does. "But I want to help at the bookstore again this week."

Tilting my head to the side, I smile warmly and, with a flourish, wave my hand across my leg. "Me and my bum foot would love that. I could really use an extra pair of hands to help." I glance over at Mary. "As long as you're not needed at the farm for anything, that is."

She shakes her head. "It'll be good for him to be at the bookstore; he really seems to enjoy it."

"I do," Duncan confirms. "I like the smell of books, when you open them and put your nose to the pages."

"Me, too, Duncan," I say with a nod. He's like a mini-me and it's cool. "I'll even spring for some fresh squeezed lemonade. Deal?"

He nods as there's a bang and slam outside the entryway. A moment later, one giant Rottweiler is barreling inside, making a beeline for me. Toto makes a quick pitstop to sniff a giggling Duncan before halting at my side.

"Can I come back and see you and Toto?" he asks. "Here. At your place."

"Well," I say with a laugh, "let me talk to Levi and see what we can do. I'm not here for very long, Duncan."

"Do you like this place, Duncan?" Levi asks as he enters the room, holding Toto's leash in one hand. When Duncan nods, Levi stands up tall. "Good, because we may move in here in a few weeks' time."

Seeing the confusion register on the little boy's face, I jump in. "Once I move out, that is, sweetie. I'm only here for a little bit while my apartment is being fixed. You'll move in after I go."

Duncan doesn't say anything; he only nods, his eyes cutting back and forth from Levi to me, over and over. Mary, seeing the break in conversation, takes the opportunity to grab his hand and usher him and Austin out the door.

"We'll leave you to get settled," she says, looking at Levi. "See you back at home?"

Levi nods, and we both watch as the small crew files out the door, leaving us alone.

Just me and Levi.

Me and my fake fiancé, hanging here together.

As he turns slowly to face me, a ripple of excitement makes its way across my flesh, causing me to shiver.

Oh, seriously. Who do I think I am?

Can I really play this part and keep my feelings in check?

ELEVEN

Levi

Standing in the middle of an aisle of the grocery store, I look down and attempt to focus on the list Georgie gave me. I'm looking at the paper, it has words, but none of them make sense to me. Nothing makes sense in my world all of a sudden.

Have you ever had a seismic shift of epic proportions happen in your life, in a very short amount of time, and you don't know how to handle it? Because this is me. This is what I'm dealing with.

Look, I've known her for the past year, more than that actually. Before I knew who she was, I had a crush on Georgie. First, she was the hottie who ran the new bookstore in town. Then, when I met her through my friend Riley, my childhood bestie who's been my ride-or-die forever, that very day I was hit with a thunderbolt of feelings to my heart center. Swear to the heavens and on my Super Bowl ring.

Getting to know her was easy; we fell into step together from the word "go." From the second she busted out her own homemade lemonade and introduced me to Toto, I was hooked. I'd go away for games, we'd text. As soon as I was back in the area, she was the person I wanted to see. We'd grab lunch and talk about what I'd seen and done, and I wanted to hear about how she was. I needed to know she was okay...and even grit my teeth as I listened to her talk about the guys she dated, too. Kind of semi-accepting I might already be in the friend zone, but in denial as well.

I round the corner of the freezer aisle and glance down at my paper: chicken fingers, French fries, and ice cream are listed. All things from this part of the store. I quickly review the list again, a little surprised there aren't any vegetables on here. Which makes me wonder: is she eating nutritiously? Maybe I should pick up a few things from the produce section. I could make her a nice salad today...also, why am I worried about her eating habits?

The sound of a woman clearing her throat behind me gives me pause. It's not like I stop anytime someone does this, but there's a tone to it that feels oddly familiar and the pitch sounds like a person who wants and needs to be seen.

I start to turn around, a shiver crawling up my spine as I do. When I see who it is, I understand my body's natural reaction.

"Lorna. Imagine running into you here." Tom's mother and the woman who wants to take Duncan from me like Atilla the Hun when he took Greece. I could engage, but I don't want to. I just want to fulfill my list and get outta here, so I open the freezer door and pull out the chicken fingers and a bag of fries.

"Bound to happen since there's only one grocery store around for miles," she says, plastering a smile across her face that is anything but heartwarming. It's tight, her features looked pinched, and I'd swear she'd had something bad to eat, but no. She's only talking to me.

She drags her eyes to my cart, judging me based on Georgie's choices, no doubt. "Chicken fingers and fries, huh?"

Tapping on the freezer door, she points to a different brand of chicken fingers. "Those are actually the ones Duncan likes."

"Good to know." I hold up the box and shake them at her. I can't help myself. "These are for someone else."

"That makes me feel better," she says with approval in her tone. Not that I need it. "There are no vegetables in your cart and I'd hate to think that my grandson's nutrition needs aren't being met while he stays with you."

While he stays with me. I could stand here and we could go back and forth, but no. Nothing good is going to come out of us conversing right now, so I start walking away. "I need to keep moving, Lorna, got a lot on my plate today."

Somehow I manage to get away from her swiftly, and I resist the urge to pat myself on my back. I want to scream at her. To ask her how dare she try to do the opposite of what her son and daughter-in-law wanted for their son. I want to ask her why? Why put us through a court case, but then I remember she is also his grandmother. She is his family, too. I have to believe she's doing this out of love for him and what she thinks, in that tiny judgy mind of hers, is best for him.

On the end cap of the aisle, I'm stoked to find that the store has a tasting table set up for new products. Am I one of those people who likes getting samples? Oh, you bet I do. My mother taught me well. I pluck up a few meatballs as I go by, the pretty cook behind the table letting me know about the barbeque sauce that's been slowly cooking all day. I take the plate she offers with more, catching her as she winks at me. I'm used to this when I'm on the road, having women flirt with me. They see a football player and…well, I can't even begin to guess what they are thinking, I just know they get really flirty and some get aggressive.

I should keep moving, but these meatballs are like witchcraft. I can't stop eating them. My fingers are covered in sauce, to the point she hands me a napkin, giggling, pointing to where the sauce is dripping down my arm. I'm delicately balancing the plate and about to say thank you and keep going, when again, a voice from behind calls out. This time it scares the bee-jeezus outta me.

"Levi." Lorna's voice cuts through the air as I lose the grip I had on my plate. It's like a slow-motion scene from a film, where we see the handsome male main character—that's me—drop a plate covered with red sauce down the front of his very white T-shirt, down his jeans, and, as the plate hits the floor and flips in the air, it sends out a spray of sauce that attacks his sneakers and socks, too.

I close my eyes and beg for strength before opening them and turning around, slowly, to face this woman. "Yes?"

"Well, that's unfortunate," she says with a smirk that could rival the Cheshire Cat's. She leans in closer so only I can hear. "I hope you're better at cleaning up messes than you are at holding onto plates."

"Touché, Lorna." I swipe a few napkins from the demonstration table and try wiping my mess. "What do you want?"

She stands in front of me, shifting her weight from one side to the other. "I'm trying to see a path forward for us, one where you'll still be able to see Duncan if you'd like, once things calm down."

I feel like she's purposely trying to get a rise out of me. You know when people do that and you can smell the manipulation?

"I don't think we should be talking, Lorna." I stare at her pointedly, gripping the cart handles as I move away. "I appreciate your efforts, but since you've taken the time to serve me with papers, I feel like we need to go through our lawyers for any communication." When she doesn't respond, I nod my head her way. "Have a good day."

Making an executive decision to get out of here, I head for the checkout line. I'd circle back and get Georgie the chocolate chip ice cream she requested, but if Mom found out I did that, I'd never hear the end of it. I make a mental note to make some for her when I get back to the farm, and surprise her with it. That way everyone wins.

I fly through the checkout; the young cashier and her friend who bags groceries do a good job of not laughing at me and my newly stained self, until they do. As the cashier slides a jug of bleach to her coworker, they exchange a look and both pairs of eyes dart my way, and teenage giggling ensues.

As soon as I pay my bill, I make a beeline for the exit. I want to get out of here before I have any more run-ins with Lorna. I should also call Buzz and let him know how she acted; it may help my side of things in the end. But even as I think this very thought, I feel sick inside. I hate going to court. I hate that we're thinking of Duncan as property, and I hate that my first instinct is to "tell on her" when in reality, she's just a sad lady who's mourning the loss of her son and daughter-in-law.

As I get closer to my SUV, I see Georgie's rolled down the window on her side of the car. Spotting me, she waves and opens the door, her jaw going slack as she sees the state of me.

"What did you spill—"

I wave a hand in the air as I click my key fob and the back of the SUV flies open. "I'll fill you in once we're out of here. Get back in the car, you won't be able to help me with your gimp self."

She laughs, then ducks back in and rolls up the window to wait. I load the bags in the back, kicking myself for not getting down the produce aisle, but add it to my list of things to do for her. I'll grab some things from our garden at the farm and bring them in with her ice cream.

"Hey, Levi." The sound of Lorna's voice is like a nail being thrust into my skull. With a giant mallet the size of Thor's hammer. While I'm fighting a migraine. "I'm sorry, but I don't think we're done."

Swiveling in place, I turn around to find her at the back of my car, the new thorn in my side, standing with her hands on her hips facing me.

"Oh," I manage, turning my back to her and tucking the last bag safely inside the truck. "Why is that?"

Her energy has changed, and she's buzzing with something more manic. A bit frenzied. I'm getting the feeling people don't usually walk away from her.

"I really think you need to look at things from my perspective. How I'm feeling about this. Me. I'm Duncan's blood." She hoists her shoulders up, standing a little taller, but to be honest, her face looks a touch crazed. "My lawyer doesn't want to go to court against you, and neither do I if we can avoid it. It's a waste of time and resources, don't you think?"

"Of course I do, but I'm not the one who lawyered up," I say.

"We can settle this out of court, you know."

Crossing my arms, I set my lips in a tight line, trying to hold back all of the anger that's beginning to well up inside of me. What a selfish woman. "That I do know. But again, I'm not the one who started this. I'm just the person who was named guardian and wants to fulfill his role that was laid out by Duncan's parents."

"That's a low blow, Levi." She shakes her head and looks haughty and disgruntled.

"No, it really isn't. I'm dedicated to doing what I need to do to make that boy comfortable and see that he's happy." Unraveling my arms, I let them hang at my sides as I shake my head at this woman yet again. "Don't you get it? I want him to have a relationship with you, I don't want him to *not* know his family. But I also want to do what Tom, and Katie, have laid out for me to do."

Lorna's cheeks are bright red, practically glowing with embarrassment or anger—I can't quite tell which. Her teeth are clenched so tightly I swear I hear them grinding together. There's a line, a tiny crease that begins to form where her brow is furrowing, and I feel like I'm watching her wind up for the pitch. Her eyes shoot daggers in my direction, invisible arrows filled with emotion, and I swear I see a faint wisp of smoke curling from her ears.

This is not a woman to be trifled with.

"You won't be any good at this, Levi. Face it. You're a man who may have resources but not enough 'oomph' to be a father."

"Oomph? You're worried I don't have oomph?" Now we're talking in tongues. "What?"

She plants herself firmly in place. "You're not even married, Levi. There's no family unit for him, how can you be a dad when you don't have a partner to help you? You're just not enough."

Her words slam into my gut and I feel a flame light way down deep inside of me. It's not a good one either. This one wants to burn the world down. My own mother raised Austin and me alone, relying on resources like Big Brothers Big Sisters to help shape us. She made sure we felt loved and whole, and as a single parent, she did an epic job. I want to react, and I'm about to. I want to say something that will cut her sharply like she's cut me, but...

"Hey." Georgie's voice breaks the heat of the moment as she limps around the truck. I say a silent thank you for her calming presence. She eyes Lorna and nods her head her way as she looks at me and taps her watch. "We need to get going, sweetie. We have that thing we need to get to."

"Yes," I say, nodding my head in time as she bobs hers, giving me a look that says trust me. "That thing."

Still ignoring Lorna, she reaches out and runs her fingers

through my hair, smiling at me. To even say that she's smiling at me feels trite; what she's doing is looking at me and she is seeing me for me, and it reflects in her eyes and her smile, in her posture and her body language.

And I'm enamored. Flummoxed. Gobsmacked. All the weird words. They are me.

"As long as you don't forget. Because to me, you're enough," she whispers, her fingers wrapping themselves around my hair as she leans in and brushes her lips across mine.

Oh, the sweet taste of Georgie tastes a lot like sweet, sweet victory mixed with the sugary amazingness of hot caramel corn. Velvety soft, like comfort foods with a flavor that lingers on the palate, leaving a trail of warmth and delight that's impossible to resist.

I could kiss her more, but she pulls away too fast. Probably because we're in the middle of a parking lot and in front of the enemy, but who knows. I'm still reeling when she holds out her hand to Lorna and introduces herself. It's a gorgeous moment that will stay burned into my memory banks for eternity.

"I'm Georgie, Levi's fiancée."

Lorna's jaw drops as Georgie's hand slips into mine. This is the moment I needed to have. It's like witnessing karma firsthand. We all know karma is there and she will get you in the end, but when we get to actually see her happening in the flesh, it is fantastic, isn't it?

But, even as I silently celebrate the moment, there's a pang of guilt. But I'll push that to the side for now, because this is what we agreed to. Friends with benefits, kind of. Different benefits than others have, but benefits nonetheless.

The bright red in Lorna's cheeks fades, turning into an embarrassed flush of pink. She takes a step or two backward, pointing herself toward the direction of the store. She stops for a brief moment, opening her mouth and closing it, choosing to wave a hand in the air as she scuttles away.

I should feel a little better than I do, but I feel...empty. I'm not combative unless I'm on the field, and then I'm getting paid to be. But me, in life, I like rolling with things and getting along with people. I like singing Broadway tunes and talking about art. I love impressionists. If I had to pick between a guy's night and an art gallery opening, I'd choose the gallery.

But me and Lorna, I don't know. Getting along may be pushing things.

"Well, my first job as your fiancée. How did I do?" Georgie asks, pulling herself away from me. She's only stepped about a foot away and I already miss her being in my space.

What is happening to me?

"If I had to give you a grade, A+ all the way. But," I point to the sauce all down the front of me, then to where it's on her now, too. "Sorry. Looks like I transferred some of my mess to you."

Her eyes dart Lorna's way before she brings them back to me. "Yes, you have, but that's okay. You know, 'cause we're engaged." She waves her hand in front of me, in a circle, a half-smile playing on her lips. "Let's get you back to the apartment so we can do something about this."

As she hobbles around the car, I can only think one thing.

I'd follow her anywhere.

TWELVE

Georgie

I kissed him. I kissed Levi. And instead of reveling in it, I'm gonna ignore it.

For now.

Instead, I'm choosing to distract myself with other things, like our engagement. Ahem, I mean our fake engagement... hmm, that sounds proletarian. Faux engagement.

Better. Whatever it takes so I DO NOT THINK ABOUT HOW SOFT THAT MAN'S LIPS ARE.

I grab my laptop out of its bag and toss it onto the ridiculously nice couch Levi bought for this place. It smells good, like ginger and peach, which I recognize. Mr. Altman traded me a few of those candles for some books recently. Of course Levi's couch smells freaking amazing. Like him.

My mind starts to wander back to those lips, but no. I need to find out how I'm supposed to act now that I'm engaged...kind of.

It's not like there's a manual for this or like I've been to any fake engagement parties over the years. I was play engaged to Tommy Woodson in the third grade, and had a wedding to one of my stuffed dolls when I was little. Does that count?

These are all questions I ask myself as I curl up on the couch with my laptop. A bang from the bathroom down the hallway causes Toto to sit up out of his afternoon slumber, eyeing me and then casting a glance in the way of the noise.

"It's Levi," I remind him. "Friend."

Toto puts his head back down as I hit return on my Google search, *I'm fake engaged now what*, while in the distance Levi sings the first few lines of "Texas Hold 'Em." I can only say, the man does not sound like Beyoncé. Judging by the way Toto's ears go flat against his skull, I don't think Levi's going to win any awards anytime soon for his voice, but we won't tell him that.

Beyoncé. Rhymes with fiancé. Where was I?

Ah yes, the internet. Leave it to Google, I find a million answers to my question. From articles about how to use being fake engaged to get discounts—which I never thought of!—to creating a gift list so people could buy your wedding gifts and stock your house...smart. Some people have faked their engagement for social media as an experiment, which sounds really funny and also awful to me, while some have done it in order to stop the other sex from hitting on them all the time.

While the latter two don't appeal, the discounts...now there's something I hadn't thought of.

I'm super curious about being marriage-adjacent, and I'd love to know what discounts are offered for brides. The last I heard, places usually hike their prices up if they find out you're getting married. Venues, cakes, catering. The cost goes up by almost twenty-five percent in some areas, and can even go up more once you say you're a bride and you're planning your wedding.

I tap on a link and get pulled down a rabbit hole of ideas: from gym memberships to trialing deejays or having bands try out for your reception. As I click and search, and read and learn the ways, Toto wanders the room, smelling all the things.

I keep one eye on him as he does, knowing he's just getting used to our temporary home.

Temporary. Everything is temporary, isn't it? Or maybe it's me. Maybe because of my childhood, I'm attracted to the temporary. My stay here, my time with Levi, the fact that I'm not really engaged to him, our time on Earth...

I shake my head. "No need to get existential," I say out loud as Toto grunts. I cast a glance in his direction to see what's interested him so much in the corner, and it's the pile of clothes Levi brought in from his truck. What are the chances he had an old bag of things he was supposed to take months ago to Goodwill still in his SUV? Chances were good, I found out, and he got lucky in finding an old pair of sweats with the Carolina Cardinals logo emblazoned across the legs and one of his mom's old sweaters.

"Georgie?" Levi calls from the shower.

"Coming!" I hop up, my original task on pause. I was supposed to bring Levi's clothes to him and throw them in the bathroom, but...sidetracked. This whole kiss thing has me spinning out. Like seeing a sparkly butterfly in the middle of a rainstorm while hanging out with Chris Martin bareback on a horse wearing a sombrero. You'd turn your head, too.

"Stay put, discount websites, I'm coming back for you," I whisper, tapping the computer and standing, my foot not hurting so much at the moment but still tender.

As I take a step toward the pile, Toto looks me in the eye as he swivels around and lifts his back leg. My mouth hangs open, and he commences in peeing all over the only set of clothes that Levi had to put on that are not stained bright red with tomato sauce.

"Toto, no!" I cry out, trying to step-clomp over to him as fast I can, not that I can do anything about it now. It doesn't help that there is a lot of urine coming out of this dog. A lot.

"Hey, Georgie, can you hear me?" Levi calls again.

I look in the direction of his voice and then back at my dog. "What have you done?"

Slowly, I make my way down to the bathroom door, step, clomp. Step. Clomp. That's me, limping in my most exaggerated way. Step, clomp. Step, clomp.

"So," I call out, leaning against the door as the water cuts off, "we've got a bit of an issue."

"What's that?" Levi's voice is muffled. He's probably under a towel. At least I had quick access to towels in my suitcase when we got back here.

"Your clothes," I peer back down the hall only to see Toto sniffing the pile as he lifts his leg again. "Toto! Stop. Lie down."

There's clamoring on the other side of the door before it swings open. I find one very wet Levi Porter standing in front of me with a towel loosely draped around his hips.

I spy abs. I spy a rock-solid chest. I spy...

"What does Toto have to do with my clothes?"

Levi shakes me out of my dazed state. Is my jaw still attached to my head? I have no words; this man is half-dressed perfection. His broad shoulders glisten with droplets of water, each muscle defined and sculpted, like a work of art. The towel hangs low on his hips, teasingly revealing just enough to send my heart racing. He moves with a casual grace, every step commanding attention. I try to tear my gaze away, but it's impossible; he's like a magnet, drawing me in with ease.

*Do not look at his body, do not look at his...*I can't help it, my eyes must be boring a hole into his abs. Movement catches my attention and I follow a trail of water as it trickles down his twelve-pack—because why bother with six?—ever so slowly and oh so deliciously headed to where the towel meets his skin.

I am not prepared.

"Hey." He chuckles, fully catching me gaping at him. "My clothes?"

"Peed on." No easy way to say it. I take a step back and try to get out of the trajectory of his Adonis-like figure. What I wouldn't do to touch one of those muscles. My eyes flick to find his dancing with what I can only describe as sheer delight.

He laughs. "You're joking."

I shake my head vigorously. Maybe too vigorous because I feel dizzy. "It wasn't me."

Levi's eyes widen and he throws his head back and laughs. His laugh is good and rich, and he's distracted so I can stare at his chest some more.

And it is nice.

"So, Toto peed on my things?" he asks.

"Sorry, it happened so fast," I say, waving my hands in the air around me. I need something to keep them busy; they feel detached from my body right now. Knitting. It's a good day to take up knitting. Keeps hands busy so they don't try to reach out and touch someone. Like Levi. "Maybe the smell of your dogs was on them?"

"That's a very real possibility," he says, bright blue eyes still sparkling. "But..." He looks down at his towel. "It leaves me with literally the towel I'm wearing."

I chew on the side of my cheek, not laughing but thinking. I snap my fingers. "I know—I've got some oversized clothes you can wear."

"You?" Levi looks my body up and down, from the top of my head to the tip of my feet. "We're not quite the same size."

I mean, he's right. I'm about five foot six, and he's gotta be pushing six foot two. "I didn't say the look would be pretty or trendy, but it'll get you home so you can get to your own things."

"Fine," he acquiesces. "Let's see what you've got."

I start my step-clomp out to the living room, headed to a suitcase I know has clothing in it, turning around when I hear the sound of feet hitting the floor behind me.

"Figured I should follow you so you don't have to double back and hobble all around," he says, smirking. "You sound like a serial killer in a Halloween movie."

"Aren't you the sweetest?" I say sarcastically, forcing a syrupy sweet Southern drawl to my words, making him smile.

I point to the suitcase where I think I have some old sweats and he pads over, opening its top. Of course the first thing he finds is one of my bras. I've got my lingerie and undergarments on the top of the pile. He pinches it between his thumb and forefinger and holds it in the air.

"Didn't peg you for purple lace, Georgie," he manages slyly.

"Give me that," I say, swiping it from his hand. I bend over and push all of my undergarments to the side, showing him where there's an old pair of sweatpants and my giant hoodie that says 'GIRLS JUST WANNA HAVE FUN' in sparkly letters that Riley gave me for my birthday last year, only it's missing the 'S' in the word 'girls' now. "There. Those things will work."

He inspects the hoodie, casting a look of doubt in my direction. "GIRL JUST WANNA HAVE FUN?"

"Hey, at least there's a fix." I say wryly. Mostly a fix for me. I need him dressed and quick cause it's a little too much for me to handle right now.

He snickers as he picks them up and, after another look my way, heads back to the bathroom to change. I hobble back down the hall with my phone in hand, praying that he comes out unassuming so I can snap a photo of him in what will have to be his worst outfit ever.

The door to the bathroom opens and he steps out. It's better than I could have imagined. The gray sweatpants are tight, pretty much not leaving anything up to the imagination if you know what I mean, and they're about five inches too short for this man's legs. He looks like a sausage stuffed in those things, but I gotta admit, his butt looks incredible.

I bet I could bounce a quarter off it.

Now, the oversized hoodie is working, but it does ride up a little. So that, combined with the fact that the sweats aren't quite up to par makes him look like he's wearing a belly shirt.

And I am here for it.

I hold up my phone, grinning, and snap a quick pic. Levi's eyes widen when he realizes what I'm up to. He takes a swipe in the air, trying to grab it from me.

"Uh-uh." I giggle, holding the phone in the air as I move backward. Note to self: don't try to run from a crime you're committing unless your feet are both in working order.

"You're injured; it's not like you can get far." He chuckles, reaching out and swiping at me again, this time his hand manages to grab my arm and stop me while his other arm wraps around my waist and he pulls me in closeandtightagainsthischestlikethis.

The air escapes me as I drag my eyes up to his. I lean backward, not able to help taunting him as I hold the phone out of reach.

"You can't really get it, can you?"

His eyes narrow. "I can get it, if I want it."

My stomach dips and dives. I want him to want *me*. That thought is something I need to deal with, but I also simply want to kiss him again. I wonder if he feels the same?

So, I test the waters. "How bad do you want it?"

I've read in my romance books about hooded eyes, but not until this moment do I understand what that means. Levi's eyes are indeed hooded and he's looking at me with an intensity that I've never experienced before with anyone, not only him.

I feel his grasp around my waist shift as he grips the back of my shirt. "Bad."

His fingers come up, raking through my hair, and I let out a heavy sigh. His lips are on my neck, hitting the tender spot just behind my earlobe as he traces a trail of kisses along my jawline and up to my lips, where he pauses.

"Is that bad enough?" he growls, pulling away.

"Could be better," I tease, standing on my tiptoes and lightly placing my lips on his, holding the kiss for a second before I pull away.

He smirks. "Trying to usurp me?"

I never have a chance to retort, his hands are in my hair as he pulls me in, slanting his lips across mine, his tongue ever so lightly tracing a line across my bottom lip. In turn, I thread my arms around his neck and pull him closer to me, wanting more.

My weight isn't quite distributed well because of my injury, and I'm trying to stay balanced. As if he senses my struggle, Levi, while expertly keeping his mouth pressed on mine, reaches down and hikes me up so he's carrying me. I'm straddled now on the front of him, our limbs tangled and our kisses sweet and searching, and we make our way back to the living room.

I am carried away and lost in this moment, not needing to come out of it, but then I remember...we have to. We're getting carried away and I like it, so it's time to slow it down. Reluctantly, I stop the magic and break the kiss, my lips tingling with the ghost of his touch.

"Hey," I say, searching his eyes as I pull back. I'm up and straightening my hair, my shirt, my everything. Wow. I am shooketh.

"Hey," he whispers, looking at me in a way he's never done before. I know a lot of people use that phrase to describe moments like this, but trust me: when it happens to you, you'll know.

Now, I do the unthinkable. I look at my watch, showing him the time. "You need to get back for Duncan, don't you?"

His eyes speak volumes, but we need to put all of this, what just happened here, on pause for a hot minute. He nods. "Yes."

I point to the front door. "Then go on and get. I do not want Mary calling you and thinking I'm holding you up."

He looks at me like he's got something to say, but instead he bites his lip and shakes his head. "You're right. I'll go clean up the bathroom and then I'm out of here."

I watch him as he exits the living room and sashays that fine ass back down the hall, shocked that I even used that term to describe him, but hey, it's a day for firsts.

Our first kiss in public for show, and our first kiss behind closed doors for...us? I know we'll have to talk about this, I know it, I do, I just don't want to. I kind of like the suspension in time of where we are, the vagueness of us. The gray area of it all. There's something comforting to me about one-sided love. It's when the feeling is returned that things get tricky.

But the kisses. THE KISSES. I could do that like it's my job. All day every day for the rest of my life.

Kissing him because I needed to for Lorna's sake is one thing, but having him kiss me and like this...child.

It's another situation altogether.

THIRTEEN

Georgie

"Gotta admit, I am in shock," Riley says, looking at me over her coffee, eyes narrowed. "This is a lot to take in in one sitting."

"You're telling me," I mumble, my eyes following Toto as he runs with Riley's dogs, Posh and Becks, down the hill of the dog park. The Sweetkiss Creek dog park is one of those green spaces that goes on for what feels like forever, complete with a well-positioned park bench, where we can sit and watch our "kids" as they play. "And all I've told you is that Duncan tried to steal a book. I'm not even warmed up yet."

Riley glances around, peering back at the parking lot. "Well, get it all out before Bex arrives."

Nodding, I sip my coffee. I had forgotten she'd invited Bex. "Okay, so you know how you picked me up from Levi's apartment today, the one that he's letting me stay in?"

She nods.

"In exchange for me staying there, we're kinda sorta— engaged." I let that word drop, and simply bring my coffee cup to my mouth and take another sip as her eyes grow wider by the millisecond. "And yesterday, we kissed. We didn't just kiss, though, we blessed that apartment with our kissing alllllll over it."

"What?" she exclaims, putting her drink down and shaking her head. "Hold on, you and Levi?"

"Also, Toto peed on Levi's clothes." I sit back and stare at my palm, pretending to be going over an invisible checklist. "Yep. I think I covered it all now."

"When I got a bingo card for this month, I didn't have any of these boxes on it," she says, letting out a giant breath with a whoosh. "How come when I was his best friend, none of these things ever happened? I turned him over to you for taking care of, and now you're engaged? I need to understand more."

I shrug as she laughs, and then a car pulling into the lot distracts us. We both turn, waving to Bex as Riley grabs my hands.

"You have to tell me more. Everything, in fact."

"Well, we're going to try to keep it quiet, only because it's not like we're really engaged." I scoot over on the bench, moving my crutches out of the way, placing them underneath us to make room for Bex.

"Who all knows?" Riley questions.

"You, me, Levi of course, his mom and Austin, and Lorna, Duncan's grandmother."

"You realize Lorna has been a Sweetkiss Creek resident for many years, right?" Riley brings up. "She's in the local bridge club and plays bingo every Saturday night at the community hall. If she knows, then all her friends know you're engaged, too."

"Who's engaged?" Bex asks as she sits down. She smiles my way. "Nice to see you again, Georgie."

"Hey, Bex." Bex is still very new to me. After moving here a few months ago, she's started to acclimate and turn up at more events around town. A former assistant for movie star, and now a Sweetkiss Creek local, Spencer Stoll, we met her through Spencer's wife, Amelia. In fact, she's the one who had messaged me and asked that I please get Bex involved with my open mic night out of the sheer fact that Amelia thinks her voice is incredible. Now, after hearing it, most of the town would agree, which is why she's got a permanent spot on the roster for Fifteen Minutes.

"I brought doughnuts." She holds up a bag and shakes it in the air, only as she does, our three dogs appear out of nowhere, making me laugh.

"First time at a dog park?" I ask as Riley giggles beside me.

"She's not a dog mom," Riley acknowledges.

Bex's eyes bounce back and forth between us. "What? What did I do?"

"First rule of the dog park: you don't bring food." Inclining my head toward the trio, who plant themselves in front of her with begging faces turned on, I grin. "Food-driven."

"Oh, man," Bex says. She goes to shove the bag inside her oversized purse, but Riley stops her.

"Nah, girl, let 'em stare. They're not the only creatures here who are food-driven. Pass me anything chocolate and filled with cream."

Bex hands her the bag and then turns back to me as she sits down on the bench beside me.

"So, engaged, huh?"

Sighing, I fill her in, too, punctuating the end of my sentence with a reminder to keep the secret. Bex holds up her hand like she's been asked to swear on the Bible. "I won't tell a soul. But, you do know that as a bride you can get, like, a whole buttload of discounts, right?"

"Yes, I do!" She's speaking my love language. "Yesterday, the internet introduced me to the world of engagement in ways I never thought or dreamed existed."

Riley laughs at me. "I've been engaged and I don't think I

received many discounts. In fact, our wedding was really expensive…but I did get free champagne when I tried on bridal dresses."

"I took note of that, don't worry." I reach into my pocket and pull out my phone, finding the list I'd saved. I tap on the note app and read. "So, two different bridal shops in town do the free champagne, I can get a discount for all of us on spa packages—if you want to be my faux bridesmaids, that is. There's bridal discounts on gym memberships and barre classes I can take, as well as a free gift from Crate and Barrel if I register with them."

I know my eyes have lit up and I'm looking a little unstable, but it's exciting. Especially if you've not ever had any of this. Just the thought of getting all of the presents makes me feel like a kid in a candy store. A small child taking in the wonder of Christmas, if you will.

Except it's all a lie. For a good reason, but still.

I let my eyes make their way over to Riley. "There's no harm in just registering, right?"

"You're going to go through the motions and pick things out for a fake wedding just to get something like a discount?"

"I'm sure Crate and Barrel would at least give me a candle. Or a picture frame," I say, watching Riley's eyes widen with each word. "Oh, come on. I won't tell anyone; only you guys will know I did it."

The pair exchange a look, Riley still shaking her head. "You just said you're trying to be careful and keep this quiet, right?"

"Right, which is why I scratched off 'putting engagement announcements in local paper.' See." I point to the phone as if I had really written it down. "It's not even here."

"You're …I don't know what you are. I'm both in awe and worried for you." Riley chuckles.

"So, does anyone want to try on dresses this week?" I

wiggle my eyebrows, letting my head spin back and forth between the two of them. "Champagne on me."

"You're literally unhinged." Riley leans around me and looks at Bex. "Do not listen to her nor let her talk you into any of it. No bueno, as they say."

Bex laughs, then turns her expression serious. "I do like a cake tasting."

She's so right. I add that to my list. "I had not thought of that..."

"Stop," Riley spits out, laughing. She kicks at my crutches under the bench. "I'll take these away so you can't go anywhere."

"I'm not an invalid, and I'm allowed to stop using them tomorrow, so that foils your plan." I take another sip of my coffee before nudging her with my shoulder. "Don't worry, I will not do any of these things."

When Riley looks at me intensely, I put a hand on my heart. "I swear."

"I'd love to know how all of this transpired so quickly," Riley says. "We haven't even discussed your make-out session."

"What?" Bex shrieks. "You made out with the hot NFL player?"

"We did, but it was more like a stress release, I think. He was in a towel, we'd been laughing—"

"A towel?" Riley's look is incredulous. "I've known that boy for years and have only seen him in swimming trunks. Never a towel."

"But were you engaged to him?" Bex asks, looking pointedly in Riley's direction as they both laugh.

"Don't be a smart-ass, Bex, you just got to town." I say this teasingly, wagging a finger at her as she holds up her hands in mock surrender. I turn my attention back to Riley. "It was a series of unfortunate circumstances that have led us to this. It's out of sheer need."

"The kissing? What did you need...mouth to mouth?"

"Breath mint check," Bex adds as Riley slaps her with a high-five.

"I think I'm done," I say, starting to stand but realizing my foot still kind of hurts, so instead, I throw myself against the back of the bench. "Are you two finished?"

"Not by a country mile," Riley purrs. "We still need to discuss where your engagement ring is. And what was it like kissing him?"

I look down at my left hand, staring at the ring finger. "I didn't even consider a ring."

"Who cares about that?" Bex chides. "Hello! What was it like when he kissed you?"

"In a word, hot." As I say it, a very wicked grin creeps across my face. "I didn't want it to stop, ever."

My hand flies to my mouth in reflex as the memory of his soft lips closing down on mine hits me like a ton of bricks. These two see it and they don't miss a beat.

"Oh wow," Bex whispers. "Did you see that? She's reacting like he just did it."

"I know," Riley acknowledges. "Your cheeks are even flushed. Wow. You're catching feelings for him, aren't you?"

"I'm not catching anything." I swat Riley's arm. "We're helping each other out."

Riley tilts her head to the side. "With kisses."

"Not just that," I argue. "With lots of things."

Riley's eyebrows lift.

I shake a finger at her. "Not those things that you're thinking about."

She winks at me as she whistles, calling the dogs back up to us. "This is a conversation we need to finish, but I gotta go pick up Jake." Jake December is her ice hockey-playing husband. His team, the River City Renegades, had been away in Canada playing a series of games and he's finally coming home for a quick break. I know this because it's all she talked about in the car on the way over to the dog park. She reaches under the bench and grabs my crutches, handing them to me.

"Thanks," I say, using them to stand up. "One more day, then all gone."

"How many people do you know have dropped their phone on their foot and ended up on crutches?" Riley asks no one in particular.

"The same number of people I've known to fake an engagement," Bex retorts. These two are on fire.

I don't say anything back, I simply hand Riley Toto's leash. She takes it from me and looks at Bex.

"Can you help me get these three dogs in the car?"

They corral our crew, and after clicking leashes onto collars, make their way over to our cars. I follow behind, taking my time. My foot may ache, but I'm not in pain like I have been, evidence of its healing. But I do let Riley's words sink in. After all, she's been Levi's bestie for reals since they were kids.

What am I doing? Am I safe? Is my heart?

Will Duncan be okay in all of this?

I'm still trying to sort out my feelings for Levi; I only know that they are big and wide, like a canyon. Or the ocean, really, as I'm beginning to realize. I've had tingles for the past year when I've thought about him, but those tingles have been replaced ever since our kiss. Now, I feel a heat rippling across me when he comes to mind. It's like I've been in a dark room for ages and someone's turned on a light. It's not really bright, but it's enough for me to see what's in front of me and has been all along.

This doesn't change that I need to prepare myself for the fact that Levi could be only in it for the way things look. Maybe he got carried away when we kissed. Maybe it's me and I was the one who got carried away. Am I a harlot? A shrew needing to be tamed? Am I probably putting too much weight on this?

Yeah. Probably.

As for getting carried away, it's something I can't be sure of until I see him next. I can only protect myself so much, but the question remains.

Can I pretend to be engaged to the man I'm falling for and not lose my heart and soul in the process?

Georgie

"How long are you going to stay online?"

Duncan's standing in front of me with his hands on his hips, looking a little perturbed. Can't lie, the stern expression he's wearing is really cute. Like adorable and precious cute.

"Can you give me one more minute?" Glancing down at the open webpage, I hold up a finger. Only two more steps and then I'll have completed my very first online bridal registry. I mean, kind of. Not that I should be, but still.

The registry I'm doing is with our local store, Altman's, and it's *only* for fun. I won't make it live, ever, I'll just save it as a draft. Something I can laugh about with Riley and Bex later this week. After yesterday's conversation, I feel like messing with them.

"One more minute," he repeats, nodding his head and narrowing his eyes. "I'll time you."

"Wow, you're a drill sergeant." He's pushy but he's excited. He's been working for me all day, and Mondays are busy because of all the deliveries we get in, so our deal is that he gets to pick out three books to take home tonight.

"I have to be. It's almost closing time and you still need to reconcile your sales so we can get out to the farm in time for dinner." Duncan crosses his arms, and I wonder where oh where has Duncan no-talk gone from just a few days ago?

"The fact that you know I reconcile my daily sales is impressive," I say with a grin, tapping away on my keyboard.

He comes over to the counter and begins to rhythmically tap his little fingers on it. Kids.

"What are those?" Duncan points to a stack of autobiographies next to me.

"These," I say, laying my hand on the top of the stack, "are for Mr. Altman. He loves autobiographies, so I always put some aside for him every month."

"What are they?"

"Stories written by people that are about them. About their life." And I wish they were currency, because I would use them as trade to refurbish my whole apartment if I could. This morning's trip down registry lane has taught me how expensive things still are. But, man, Levi's place is really making me want the nice things in life.

Just a few more clicks and I'll be able to close down my computer. I look back over my list, laughing at the ridiculous giant metal ostrich I picked out. Toto would flip out if that thing showed up at my place. The list is full of things I really would love to have, but mostly really weird things that a very particular person would be after. I'm not saying these things are hideous or that they're stupid, they're items that are just not me. But that's the point, I just want to freak out my friends.

"People like reading about other people's lives?" Duncan asks, pulling my attention back to him.

"They do. Celebrities have some good autobiographies. There's one written by Prince Harry that was really popular last year."

"Do you have to be popular to write one?"

"No," I respond, my eyes still on the screen. Babysitter of the year right here. Or would I be a stepmother? "You don't have to be popular nor well known to write your autobiography."

"Just have a cool life, right?"

"In my mind, all of us have a cool life. We all have a story."

"Do you have one?" Dark eyes bore holes into me.

"I do." I stop what I'm doing momentarily to focus on Duncan. "Not a lot of people know I was in the foster system in New York when I was little."

"What does that mean?"

"I never knew my parents, and I was placed in different homes all the time with strangers who would take care of me. I used to pray that I'd be adopted into a perfect family, like the Porters seem to be, but it never happened."

Duncan nods his head, biting his lower lip. "So you didn't have your parents around, like me?"

"Kind of," I say with a smile, reaching out to squeeze his forearm. "I had other adults who contributed to taking care of me, but not my blood parents. I didn't know them at all, but that's okay." I hold my hands up as if I'm showing him the room for the first time. "All of that made me stronger, so I could work really hard and make this happen. Have something like the bookstore that's all mine."

I can tell he's hanging on to my words, realizing the roots of our kinship at the same time I do. There's a little bond happening here, and I never want to betray this guy. As he goes quiet, I leave him with his thoughts and go back to chuckling at my registry, but also making sure I've not ticked off any boxes, accidentally making the page live for anyone to be able to see.

"Do you think you want to be a mom?"

My eyes snap up to Duncan's in a millisecond. "Huh?" I

reply, as if he just asked me if I wanted to join the circus and learn to juggle flaming torches.

"Like, would you be a mom even though you don't have one?"

I'm literally chewing on the inside of my cheek so I don't giggle out loud. "Probably, but I've not ever thought about it."

We're going deep quickly for a ten-year-old. How can I change this subject? I nod at the pile of autobiographies beside me, but turn my attention back to the laptop. "Hey, do you want to check one of these out?"

Duncan's eyes light up. I love how into books this kid is. "Yes, please."

With my eyes still on the computer, I reach out for one of the books on the stack. I grab the top book and go to pass it off to Duncan, only as I do, I lose my grasp on it and it tumbles from my hand, knocking into my coffee mug from this morning, which is of course not empty, sending liquid all over the counter.

"No!" Both of my hands slam down on the keyboard in surprise as I take the laptop off the counter, tossing it on a box beside me. Duncan and I both grab books and anything that could get damaged and move them out of the way as fast as we can. After a few minutes of full-on scrambling, we both stop, facing one another with our eyes wide.

"That could have been a disaster," Duncan confirms.

"You bet it could have been, but you acted fast." I ruffle his hair. "That's a lesson for you. This is why we should always use cups and mugs with lids around here. In fact, I'll make sure to get us a couple so this doesn't happen again."

"Cool." Duncan grins, nodding at my computer. "Is that okay?"

Flipping it over, I quickly inspect it, only to find the bottom of my old 2015 MacBook Air is coated with coffee. Grabbing a towel, I wipe it while praying that it's not dead.

This poor thing has been on its last legs for ages, and this could be the final straw. I open the cover and the screen, once bright and full of zest, and a bridal registry, is now blank.

I shift my gaze to Duncan. "Well, it doesn't look good."

"My mom dropped her phone in the toilet once and she made it work again by putting it in a bag of rice."

While it sounds like a good fix, I doubt it could help my situation, but hey. You never know. "Really? Should we try that when we get to the farm?"

Duncan's eyes sparkle. "I'll do it for you!"

"Okay." I chuckle, handing him the computer. "You're in charge of it." I look at the time, pointing to the front door as I do. Mary had dropped Duncan off this morning for his "shift." When she did, she asked if I minded driving him back out, which of course I can, especially since today I'm officially off the crutches, and she'd asked if I'd like to stay for dinner. "Flip the sign from open to closed, and you can pick out your books while I close out."

Had she made a side comment about it being my engagement dinner? She did, but she'd punctuated the awkward moment with a cheeky grin, too. I'm no stranger to dealing with awkward moments, I know how to sidestep 'em and change the subject like nobody's business. As soon as I told her how much I loved her homemade peppermint stick ice cream, I could see her literally puff up with pride right in front of me. What can I say, I know where my bread is buttered, if you know what I'm saying.

Actually, I know where my ice cream is getting scooped—at least, where I'd like it to be, and I want to keep that ice cream coming. If it also allows me to maybe talk to Levi since we haven't had a chance to be in person since last week, then that's the cherry on top of the peppermint stick sundae.

"But it was Easter, did you really hide both baskets so well that they never found them?"

Family mealtime with the Porters is exactly as much fun as you'd think it would be. Duncan and I arrived just as Mary pulled her famous homemade lasagna from the oven, corralling all of us into the dining room almost immediately. All of this leaves no time for me to pull Levi aside and at least address the lips-on-lips situation from a few days ago.

Mary tries not to spit out her sweet tea. "Look, I was tired that day and wanted these two to stay busy. I'd been up working in the fields with the dogs all morning before they even got out of bed that year...let's remember I was also a single parent."

"Oh, boo-hoo," Austin teases, fake punching his mom in the arm. "You had us two strong boys around, you didn't need anything else."

"I needed an adult." She laughs. "At the time, I couldn't even remember hiding those baskets. I was that tired, so when they came in after looking for them for most of the morning and had nothing, I was no help."

"You didn't remember where you left their baskets?" I'm holding my side picturing the look on a young Levi's face when he couldn't find his present from the Easter Bunny. Eyes wide, lips in a tight line, feet firmly planted in frustration.

"You think that's funny?" Levi says from his seat beside me, poking me in my ribs. "We did eventually find those baskets."

I spin in my seat to face him. "When?"

Austin bursts out laughing. "Three years later at the top of the barn in the loft, buried in the hay. They were moldy and half-eaten by wild animals."

The table erupts in laughter; even Duncan's giggle joins the chorus, making both Levi and I grin as we exchange a look of pride. There's a stabbing in my stomach as this happens, as if a cautionary warning reminding me that this is all fun, and while this family dynamic is amazing, in the end I'm the part of this story that doesn't fit.

Three of these things belong together, one of these things is not the same...

"Who wants dessert?" Mary asks. Duncan and Austin both raise their hands in the air, Duncan giggling when it happens.

"Okay, then. Austin, you're on ice cream duty. Hey, Duncan," Mary says as she pushes her chair back, "help me clear the dishes?"

Wordlessly, Duncan does as he's told, following Mary into the kitchen as Austin does the same, turning back to wink at Levi and me as he exits the room stage right. Leaving us alone for the first time since all the yummy kisses.

"So." I turn in my seat, facing Levi. "He asked me if I wanted to be a mom today."

Levi, who had been taking a drink of his tea, chokes. "He what?"

Slowly I nod, my shoulders shaking with laughter. "He's pretty smart that kid, more than we probably give him credit for."

Levi's eyes stay trained on the door leading to the kitchen. "I worry about him finding out about this whole thing."

"Which thing? The court case with him at the center, or the part where we're engaged but not really?"

"Both," Levi responds, looking at his hands as they twist in his lap. "He's really opening up. The way he's communicating with all of us is slow going, but it's happening. I know a lot of that is the trust you two have."

I shrug. "But he needed time to settle in, too."

"He'll start therapy this week," Levi whispers, his eyes locked with mine. "I'll go with him but just be there in case he wants me in the room."

Instinctively, my hand reaches out for his. "Good. I'm glad you're doing that for both of you."

His eyes drop to where my hand covers his, and he smiles. In the next room, there's a commotion and laughter as Austin does something to make Duncan giggle, his laugh like a melody.

"I feel like I need to ask you how you're doing after the other day." Levi's eyes slam into mine. He drops his voice an octave, gripping my hand tighter. "Because I can't stop thinking about kissing you."

The things I'm not prepared for in life are few. Earthquakes go on the list because we're in North Carolina. Being invaded by pirates, too, since we're in the mountains and not on the coast.

We can also add Levi Porter giving me sexy, hooded eyes again as he tells me he can't stop thinking about kissing me to that list as well.

My hand flies to my lips as a low heat hits my cheeks. "I know I'm totally blushing right now."

He smiles, this lazy, beautiful, sexy grin that drips from his lips as he looks at mine, taking his time bringing his eyes north. "You are, but that color pink looks mighty fine on you."

His hand squeezes mine and a warmth fills my belly. Warm from the food, from the family time, from the love in this room when all the Porters are in it, and for sure one hundred percent warmth and fire and heat from the fact that this man is hitting all the right notes.

"Are we doing the right thing here, Levi?" I say in a whisper.

He stares at me for only a brief moment before he takes my hand and raises it to his lips, kissing the back of it as he keeps his eyes on mine.

"I hope so." He gently puts my hand back down, staring at where our hands are tangled in my lap. "Because I really like kissing you, Georgina Simpson. And I really want to do it again and soon."

I'm overwhelmed with the giddiness that flows through my body; there's, like, ten thousand sparks of energy that are flicking off and on inside me. Part of me wants to revel in all of this, just enjoy the ride and see where it takes us, but the other part of me is so nervous. My heart feels like it's doing the Macarena, skipping beats and then racing ahead. I can't seem to stop the silly grin that's spreading across my face, nor do I want to. It's like my whole world just got a Technicolor makeover, and I'm living in a rom-com montage.

But underneath the excitement, there's a hint of fear, a nagging voice in the back of my mind asking, "What if this changes everything?" This man has become one of my good friends, and if we don't do this right, that could go away. There's also Duncan, and we need to keep him a priority as well. After all, he's the one all of this is for, right?

I let my other hand find its way to his jawline, stroking it slowly with my forefinger. This man doesn't have a chiseled jaw, it's sculpted to perfection, and I let my fingertips dance as I lean closer to him. My fingers find his lips, slowly stroking them as he closes his eyes.

"You're making me crazy," he growls, his lips beginning to curl upwards. "Is it time for me to kiss my fake fiancée again or are there limits?"

I'm about to open my mouth to respond when a tiny, familiar voice suddenly pipes up.

"What's a fake fiancée?" Duncan asks.

FIFTEEN

Levi

"Do you think Georgie's open mic night was good last night?"

Duncan has not spoken to me as much as he has in the past two days in the whole time I've known him. Since Georgie was here for dinner, he's been chattering nonstop about the bookstore, about her computer he tried to fix by sticking it in a bag of rice, and about Toto. There was also a soliloquy about autobiographies which I didn't understand and, oh, yeah.

Questions about what a fake fiancée means.

"Want to call and ask her how it was?" I hand him my phone. "I'm sure she'd love to hear from you."

Duncan takes the phone, eyes it, and puts it on the counter. "Nah. I don't want to look thirsty."

"Thirsty." I swallow a laugh. Who knew ten-year-olds could be so precocious? "I don't think she'll see it as thirsty, buddy. Just curious."

"Maybe you want to call her," he challenges, crossing his arms.

"If I do, I'll just call her." I look up from the paperwork

I'm not-so-fully engrossed in and point to the ping-pong table in the middle of the barn. "Want to play a game when I'm done?"

Duncan nods. "Sure. Then next time Georgie's out, she can play the winner."

Putting my pen down, I put Duncan in my sights. Time for a man-to-man talk. "You know, I noticed that from the moment you got to know her, you've been super attached to Georgie. Is there a reason why?"

Duncan shrugs as he picks up a ping-pong ball and starts to tap it with a paddle, keeping it under control as he chats with me. "Dunno."

"You don't know or you don't want to tell me?" When I see his eyes shift around the room, I give him further permission. "You can have a secret with her if you want and not tell me, but if you can let me know, I'd really like it. I want us to have the kind of relationship where you can come to me to talk about anything, Duncan. Everything. I'm not perfect, but maybe I can help, too?"

He's quiet and reflective before he speaks. "Did you know she's an orphan?" he asks thoughtfully as he catches the ball and stops tapping it repeatedly.

I nod, understanding coming over me. "She told me about her childhood."

"She's alone, like me. She gets me." His eyes widen as he says the words. "Not that you don't, it's only that she's different."

"It's fine," I say, standing up and walking over to the table to join him. "I want you to know my door is always open for us to talk; you tell me when and where, and I'm there. And if you want to talk to Georgie, you talk to her." I wait a beat before I press on. "Also, you're not alone, Duncan. You've got us now. Me, my mom, and Austin. We're here for you. Always."

Duncan goes quiet, but his eyes say so much. I can see the fear, the worry, the lack of understanding yet also fully knowing and comprehending what's going on around him. When he had asked us about the fake fiancée comment two nights ago, we'd quickly covered our bases. Georgie had insisted it was a movie she'd seen, and he'd let the comment slide under the rug.

This time.

"Look..." I kneel in front of him. "You've been through something in your life that none of us will ever understand, so I'm making an appointment for us to go talk to someone."

His eyes light up. "Georgie?"

"No." I chuckle, shaking my head. "He's a therapist, a man in town who you can talk to about how you feel and about your parents."

Duncan's brow furrows. "But you just said I can talk to you and Georgie."

"You can, but this man will help you talk about losing your parents and how to handle those feelings. I'm going to go to see him, too, so that way we can all talk about it." I push his bangs off his forehead, Georgie's comment about him needing a haircut hitting home. "If you're okay with me going, too, that is."

He slowly nods, big brown eyes finding mine. "Will I have to talk about why I don't want to live with Grandmom?"

Well, this is news. "You can, if you want."

I stay still, not wanting to press him. The barn is quiet except for the occasional snore coming from one of the four truffle dogs that are in here with us sleeping. The small crew is usually with my mom when she's here, but since she's out running errands today, they followed Duncan and me to the barn.

"I don't want to live with her," he says, his voice small. "But I don't want her to be sad that I'm not there."

I feel a touch guilty for a second, but it does feel good to be the chosen one. "Feel like talking about why you don't want to live with her?"

"Well, she doesn't have a farm," he says with all seriousness. "I mean, I know she wants me there, but I can't be. She's very sad all the time and wants to talk about what happened over and over again."

"You don't want to do that?"

He shakes his head from side to side. I can only imagine what it must feel like for all of them to relive the hurt from last year over and over, but for Duncan to have to when he's the sole survivor has to be gut-wrenching and impossible to understand when you're ten.

"Well, when you start to see your therapist he'll help you create boundaries so you can talk about what you want and need, okay?" I lean down and pull him in for a hug, not expecting anything in return. However, I'm surprised and buoyed when he wraps his hands around my waist and squeezes me tight.

"I don't want her to be mad, I just want to be...here."

"It's fine, and we'll figure it out, okay? It's not like any of us have been through this before."

"I still want to see my grandmom, just not live with her." His voice is so matter-of-fact, like "Why can't you adults do it like this?" This kid is so gonna run for President one day. Fingers crossed.

"Well, the next time I see her, we'll talk about this, okay?"

"I don't have to do it?"

"No, I can," I say as I ruffle his hair.

"Cool." He shoves his hands in his front pockets. "So, I know you want to play ping-pong but...can I go play video games for a little while instead?"

Go figure. My head is spinning from all the turns this conversation is taking. "Go for it."

He cracks me up as he skips out of the barn. Even the dogs are pulled in by his energy as they all rise from their slumbers and trot behind him, following him back to the house.

I wonder if this is what parenting really looks like. Trying to find a gray area in keeping kids young and oblivious while also gently bringing them into a very adult world with very adult situations. Social media, mobile phones, dating.

Sighing, I scratch my head as I sit back down and stare at the paperwork I'd discarded earlier. A letter of retirement I've been working on with my agent, Travis, to give to the owner of the team letting everyone know that next year is officially my last year in the NFL playing professionally. I'm still not one hundred percent sure that this is what I'm supposed to do, so it's not gone to anyone yet. I've not talked to anyone except Travis about this because I just don't know if it's what I'm doing yet.

When I think about my career, I've had a good run. An amazing one. From high school state championships to college wins, and now a career that has taken me places I never thought I'd end up.

But now, there's Duncan.

Now, there's also Georgie—and there's a possibility of a future with both.

Just the thought of her brings a grin to my face that is a mile wide. When I think about her, I think about that kiss in my apartment. The other night at dinner, I fought my instinct to drag her out of the room and press her up against a wall and slam my mouth across hers.

Yet, Duncan's words also reverberate in my ear. *She's alone. Like me.*

I was able to explain to him that he's not alone, and I know he gets me, but does Georgie think that, too? Does she feel alone in the world?

I put the documents back in their folder for safekeeping. I can come back to them another day.

Instead, I let images of Georgie dance in my mind, the feeling of those soft, full lips still imprinted on me. I've wanted to kiss her for so long, and to finally have it happen, well, I'm a little embarrassed she had to be the first one to do it. But I'm catching up, slowly. From what I can tell from our brief conversation at dinner the other night, she's on the same page. Which is good. Great in fact.

Because I'm starting to see a life without her in it may not be a fun one at all. Over the last few days, I've checked in with myself, wondering if I could date someone else who isn't Georgie or if I could be interested in someone down the road. The answer is always the same as it has been since I met her: a resounding no.

When I think about seeing her with someone else, something absolutely insane happens inside of me. I feel like steam starts to come out of my ears and I want to scream. The thought of another man even touching her...

But she's not really mine to have, is she? We're *quid pro quo*. Or are we?

"Argh!" I shake my head and stand up from the desk. The gym is calling. When I'm this pent-up, I need a good workout.

It would appear that by asking for this favor I've gotten me and Georgie right tangled in a web of untruths. But does it count if I'm starting to fall head over heels for her?

Georgie

"Do you have anything on the Roman Empire?"

Tilting my head to the side, I purse my lips and put on my thinking face. Or at least my best impression of what I think one looks like. "So it's true that men think about the Roman Empire at least once a day, huh?"

The cute customer, who has been keeping me busy for the last ten minutes looking for books that I swear do not exist, smiles at me. It's a great smile, perfect actually. Like he could be in a commercial for toothpaste and wouldn't have to even get his teeth whitened for it; they're that on point. I swear he's flirting with me, but I honestly can't be sure. I don't even know what flirting is anymore; I only know what making out with Levi feels like and it's probably the closest I'll ever get to heaven.

"I probably think about it twice a day," he says, placing both hands on the counter as he treats me further to his lopsided grin. "I've got history classes at Appalachian State."

Ah, young and cute. And a student. He's also the man standing in between me and an afternoon of trying on bridal dresses.

"So it's required reading?" I ask, and he shakes his head no.

"I'm a professor," he says with a little flair as the front door of the shop opens. The professor doesn't bother turning around to see who's entered the room; he only keeps his eyes trained on me. Yep, he's definitely flirting.

When I pull my eyes from his to greet my new customer, I'm a little shocked when I discover Levi standing at the door, the handle still in his grasp as he stares at the man in front of me. I watch as his other hand flexes, opening and closing into a fist, and it makes me a little...happy? Younger Georgie would be telling Future Georgie to stay away from a man who seems to have a temper, but in this case, I know this man and he's showing me something I didn't think he had in him —jealousy.

Green is so not his color, but I can't help but dig it. Just a little. A huge grin immediately washes across my features; I can feel my cheeks swelling.

"Hey!" I wave. "Wasn't expecting to see you."

In a matter of seconds, Levi is behind the counter and placing an arm around me, brushing his lips against my cheek. "Wanted to surprise you, sweetie."

I watch as Levi's eyes slide over to the professor and he holds out his hand. He goes to introduce himself, but the professor is already in his own state of shock and awe.

"You're Levi Porter!" He takes Levi's hand and pumps it furiously. "Dude. Your Super Bowl game this year was epic! It's so cool to meet you."

Levi's energy shifts almost instantaneously as the pair chat away, the whole standoff ending with Levi scribbling an autograph on a piece of paper and the professor buying two books from the "TikTok Made Me Buy It" table at the front.

"What are you doing here?" I ask as the customer leaves. "I was about to close up for the day and meet Bex."

"Duncan's got therapy, so I'm killing time." He cocks his head to one side. "What are you and Bex doing?"

Do I tell him that I'm trying on wedding dresses so I can get a free drink and a gift card for a mani pedi? No.

"We're going...shopping." Technically, not a lie.

His eyes narrow. "You're closing up early to go shopping?"

Grabbing my bag, I point to the clock. "Only an hour early, and it's a Friday. I've had a busy week."

He follows me to the door and out onto the sidewalk while I lock up. When I turn around, he's standing right behind me. So close I can basically taste his breath.

"We need to find time, me and you, to talk." A lone finger begins tracing its way across the back of my hand. "We didn't quite get a chance to finish our conversation, thanks to little ears."

"Did you have to explain anything about fake engagements?"

Levi shakes his head. "Your cover that we were talking about some plot point for a movie worked, but he still wanted to know why people would do it."

I wince, but only slightly. "Well, we need to be extra careful with him around."

"I'm not going to argue with you since the hearing is in a few weeks. There's still time for him to find out that we're being, shall we say, devious. Call me crazy, but as his role model, I don't want that to happen."

"Noted," I say, laughing. As I do, I realize his eyes are fully focused on my mouth. He is staring at my lips, hard, and I pat myself on the back for exfoliating them this morning. A girl has to do what a girl has to do.

Not to let the moment pass, I test the waters and lick them, his sigh evidence that I did catch him in the act. One of his fingers twirls through the belt loop on my jeans as he pulls me close.

Everything inside of me hitches and seizes as he slowly and tenderly places his lips on top of mine, right here, out in front of Pages and Prose. Right here on Magnolia Lane for all the world, and Mr. Altman, to see. Right here, across the street from Lorna.

I stop and pull away, but Levi's hand stays on the small of my back.

"Lorna's over there," he manages with a grumble.

"I know," I retort. "With a group of her friends."

He leans back in so we're cheek to cheek. "Just stay put for a moment longer, okay?"

I know it's silly and I shouldn't think this way, especially after the man was telling me at his family's dining room table just the other night how he wanted to kiss me again, but...a little bit of the fire that's been flaming during this moment gets extinguished when I see it's all for show.

But I have to keep my part of our bargain. I have a place to stay and he has a stable bride-to-be. Stable being the operative word, obviously. So, I lean into it and make a show of things right back. I press my lips harder against his and let my hands come to the side of his face, my left hand cupping his cheek before I pull away.

"How's that?" I ask, not wanting to look and see if Lorna's still there.

Levi's eyes flick across the road. "Good. And she's gone, so I'm sure we made our point."

I tuck that comment away, choosing to ignore it and the feelings I'm having right now. I need to meet Bex.

After what felt like hours, but in reality was only about ninety minutes, I walk out of Sweet Serenity Bridal with my arm looped through Bex's, laughing. We'd managed to have about two glasses more champagne than I'm used to, but it made the fashion show we just endured that much sweeter.

"So, we learned today that a ball gown is not your thing, you're not a Cinderella type, and that you rock a tea-length dress." Bex giggles. "Also, lace is not your friend."

"No, it's not. The texture makes me crazy." I cringe. "Always has and always will, I guess."

"I'm hungry." Bex taps her stomach. "I did not foresee having so much to drink. Want to grab some food?"

The thought of a bowl of fries in my mouth right now is amazing. "Yes, please."

As we make our way down the street arm in arm, reminiscing about the vintage number Bex tried on (which would be a great bridesmaid dress *if* I was really getting married), my phone beeps. Ignoring it, we press on, heading for the nearest cafe.

But my phone has other ideas. It beeps again, and again. Then once more. Then it beeps again. Finally, Bex stops in her tracks, pulling me to a sudden halt alongside her.

"Will you look at your phone? Someone is obviously trying their hardest to get ahold of you."

Rolling my eyes, I grab it from my purse and am shocked at the amount of notifications I have. I'm not sure what to check first, so I start with the texts telling me that packages are being delivered to my house.

Quickly I scroll through them, wondering what these items are that are showing up, only to have a pang of fear shoot through me.

"Oh no," I whisper-shriek as I open my email, cross-checking the items with a little list I had flagged in my saved emails. "That registry page was supposed to stay private!"

Bex's head almost spins off her neck. "Did you end up making a registry?"

"Yes." I wince. "I just wanted to try it out, maybe laugh

about it with you and Riley, but I thought I kept the page private." I turn my phone around to show her, via my security camera app, the small pile of boxes at the back door of the bookstore. "Looks like someone got me some of the smaller home items that I had on the list?"

Bex's hand barely makes it to her mouth to cover it before she barks out a laugh. Good for you, Bex. You can laugh for both of us because I'm horrified.

"This is not good." That's all I can manage as I head for a nearby bench to sit down. I need a second to think, and those two extra glasses of bubbly are not helping me. I close my phone and sit quietly, wondering how I'm going to explain this side of me and what I've done to Levi. The side that's a little nutty, the one that wanted to know what it felt like to just let it all ride and get some presents.

"It's fine," Bex says, sitting beside me. "We'll go by the store, get the boxes, and take them back to...where did you get them from?"

"Altman's."

Bex smacks my arm. "You went through a local business? I've not been here that long and I know that you don't do that. It's Small Town 101."

Grimacing, I look her way. "What's that supposed to mean?"

"That the whole town probably knows you have a registry." She shakes her head as she attempts to swallow back her laughter. "Girl. What have you done?"

I'm still trying to find an answer when my phone dings again. Glancing down, I'm reminded there's some social media posts I've been tagged in that I need to look at. Tapping open the app for that, for the second time in five minutes my jaw slams on the sidewalk.

"Now what?" Bex asks, taking the phone from me, only to have her jaw mimic mine as she sees the photo.

There I am, in front of the bookstore with Levi, in a full clutch. His lips on mine, my hands in his hair. Someone's posted two photos: one of us embracing and the other a close-up of my left hand, with a bright circle around my ring finger.

"Ooof," Bex acknowledges.

"What is this?" I ask no one in particular, forgetting that I am sitting with an ex-celebrity personal assistant.

"It's a gossip account," she says with full confidence. "Seen this one before. People send them pictures so they post them on their behalf. Like *Gossip Girl* but with more visuals."

"So I'm the gossip."

"Yes and no," she says as she reads the caption accompanying the picture. "Looks like whoever took this photo also hunted around and found your bridal registry, so the cat is out of the proverbial bag."

Groaning, I fold over, putting my elbows on my knees and my head in my hands. "Oh, not good. Duncan is going to find out."

"Duncan? Everyone is going to find out. And"—she points to the photo—"the people want to know where your ring is."

Things you don't think about when planning your quickie fake engagement. "Maybe I don't wear it because it's so expensive."

"If you had one," Bex reminds me with a chuckle.

"Yes. There's that, too." Taking the phone from her, I scroll through the comments, reading them. Not sure why I thought that would be a good idea, but for Future Georgie, I need someone to tell me to never do this again.

"What is this?" I point to the comments. "This person says, 'What? She's not even wearing makeup?' And this one: 'She's not as pretty as I thought his fiancée would be.' What is that about?"

"Ignore it," Bex says with authority. "Keyboard warriors

trying to get a rise out of you." She takes the phone from me. "You're not allowed to read any more, not until you talk to Levi. I've been down this road so many times with Spencer and Amelia. The way the fans used to treat her when they got together was horrible. I bet you could talk to Riley about what she's dealt with being married to one of the AHL's most famous hockey players. It's not for the faint of heart."

I know she's right, but I don't want to deal with any of it right now. Or ever, for that matter. I sigh as my phone dings. Again.

"You just got another present delivered. Looks like a giant metal bird. An ostrich maybe?" Bex mutters as I kick my foot out. Why did I have to add that ostrich to my gift registry?

"How come no one explains to you that this is par for the course? The part where people think they know you and can talk about you like that?" Still with my head in my hands, I keep my eyes on the sidewalk as I talk. "No one told me that being a fake fiancée was going to be so mentally taxing."

"So, it's fake, huh?" a voice that is not Bex's bellows.

Slowly, I raise my head, my stomach turning a million somersaults, finding Lorna standing in front of me with her hands on her hips. Of course she would be here. I saw her just two hours ago on this very street, so the likelihood of her still being in the area is...well, odds are good 'cause she's standing in front of me, isn't she?

"I asked you a question," she says, crossing her arms as she stares at me with vengeance and anger in her eyes. "Is your engagement to Levi fake?"

I start to nod but then shake my head. In the end, I choose to shrug. I feel like this could become my signature move. I'll call it the "yeah-nah-maybe." "It's complicated."

"Is it, though?" she snaps.

"If she's saying it is—" Bex begins, but I pat her knee to call her off.

I stand up, clasping my hands together in front of me. "I really don't think we should have this conversation right now, Lorna."

"Then when can we have it?" She unravels her arms, agitated, and puts her hands back on her hips. "If you and Levi are lying to make him look good, this won't go down well with the judge. I can tell you that much. And what kind of example are you setting for Duncan?"

Things I've asked myself Lorna, but I won't dare to say this part out loud.

I hold my hands in front of me to hold off her verbal assault. "Please. I think you should talk to Levi about this."

"Why do that when you're here now?" She stays where she's planted herself, holding herself more rigidly.

I can't do it. It's not that I'm done, but I'm crumbling. Duncan, the social media post, the comments, the feelings for Levi and the kisses, the presents showing up and me going absolutely bonkers for all the discounts, and now this. I'm at a breaking point with this whole thing. I'm just not made for it, I guess.

We may be busted, but at least I can still stick up for my best friend. Could my words be slightly fueled by champers? Yup.

"Lorna, have you ever stopped to think that he might not be faking anything if you would just simply comply with the wishes of your son and his wife?" My voice is pleading but stern. Even as amped-up as I am on the inside, I can keep my empathy at the forefront. "Levi wants to do what's best for Duncan, and he wants to honor Tom and Katie's wishes. Why can't you see that?"

"Does he think that faking his marriage is what is best for an impressionable young man?" She huffs, shaking her head. "Nope, this is ridiculous. That child needs to live with me."

"You just want to win, don't you?"

She nods as I stare at her. Unbelievable.

I try to keep my tone steady, but it's incredulous. "Lorna, I think you need to look deep into your heart of hearts and ask yourself one question. Can you do that for me?"

She rolls her eyes, but she doesn't speak.

"What would your son want?" When she drops her gaze to the ground, I push on, but I'm a little riled up and wagging my finger now, too. "We both know because he's already stated it. Levi is Duncan's godfather and he's going to make a great guardian. Fantastic one, really. You know when I was little, all I wanted was to have a family. A solid one that loved me for me and was there to support me and hang out for holidays, to show up when I was in the school play or got an award. To be at the talent show the year I got in for playing the flute. I was a foster kid and, unfortunately for me, I was one of the ones who never got to know what it's like to grow up in a home like you probably created for your son, that Mary has made for the Porter boys, and like the home, fake fiancé or not, that Levi is going to give to Duncan."

I stay in my place for a moment to see if she's going to react. When she keeps her stare focused on the ground, I take it as my cue to go.

Turning around, I flick a hand in the air at Bex.

"You ready?"

Bex nods, and Lorna raises her head, a new fire of determination igniting behind her eyes.

"That was a nice try, but..." She reaches in her bag and pulls out her phone. "Between the alcohol I smell on your breath and that whole display you just treated me to, I'm having more doubts about where my grandchild will end up. I need to call my lawyer."

Lorna then pivots on her heel and flounces away as Bex's arm snakes around my shoulder and she pulls me close. A feeling of sheer horror ripples through me.

What have I just done?

SEVENTEEN

Levi

For the last ten minutes, I've listened to Georgie, without speaking, as she explains to me about her run-in with Lorna. My ear is sweating, we've been on the phone so long. Combine that with the allergy attack I'm having thanks to the cat sleeping in my room again, and I'm a hot Southern-fried mess.

Every other sentence, she stops to say she's sorry, over and over, for being the one who let this slip, "and in front of all people, it had to be Lorna." She's riding a turbulent wave of emotions, and it's all my fault.

She should know I can't blame her. I'm the one who asked her to do this with me. For me. To "scratch my back and I'll scratch yours." It's like she's Julia Roberts and I'm Richard Gere and I've forced her into this situation by saying I'd give her a place to stay if she just pretended that she was marrying me. I've managed to pull a *Pretty Woman* on my best friend.

By the time I hang up, she's calmer, but not by much. She has every right to be upset, but not at herself. At me. I'm the problem here.

I can hear Mom and Austin out on the porch, and the sound of a television set blaring upstairs lets me know that Duncan's assumed his position playing video games. Once he's been here longer, I'll put more boundaries up around his screen time, but these days I simply want him to want for nothing.

Dialing Buzz, I question if that was a good idea in the first place, because wanting Duncan to only have the best has led to this moment. I let the phone ring and ring until finally Buzz's voicemail picks up. How can I sum up everything I have to say succinctly and quickly in a fast message?

The answer to this is: I can't. Instead, when his voicemail picks up, I can only beg him to call me back before disconnecting and throwing open the door to the porch. Time to talk to my people about this mess I've created.

"What happened to your face?" Austin asks, his jaw hitting the ground when I walk out, causing Mom to spin around from her seat only to stare at me in shock as well.

"Sweetie," she says, rising to come over and look at my puffiness in all of its glory. "That stinking cat loves you so much."

Another reason to move out soon, but I don't say it out loud. "And I love Snickers, too, but that cat cannot come into my room anymore."

"At least your bride-to-be is a dog person," Austin says, making an attempt at humor but not realizing the mood I'm in. He catches on when I glower and look his way. "What's going on? You don't look like you're in a good place."

"Because I'm not in a good place," I growl, filling them in on Georgie's run-in with Lorna. It takes me a hot second to cover everything Georgie shared, but I get there in the end. As soon as I'm done, I pull a chair out from our outdoor patio table and spin it around so I can face these two and hopefully hear some good advice.

Austin's the first to react. "Wow, Levi. I don't even know what to say."

Okay. Austin's got nothing. I turn and look at my mother, who shakes her head.

"I didn't think this was going to end well," she says, but her voice is filled with understanding and not as much "I told you so" as I was expecting. "Have you called Buzz?"

"Did that before I came outside." I slam myself into the chair and stare at the sky. "This is going to hurt my chances of getting Duncan, isn't it?"

"Only Buzz can tell you that," my mother shares, patting my leg. "I keep thinking that, of course, the courts will see that you get Duncan because of Tom's wishes, but..."

She doesn't have to say what she's thinking. I'm thinking about it, too. If I hadn't lied like this, I would have made a stronger case.

I know that most of this is out of my hands and it's up to the courts. I knew that going into this. So why did I freak out and insist on saying anything to Georgie? Why would I ask her to pretend to be engaged so I could make sure I got custody of Duncan?

Because it's what your friend wanted, for you to take care of Duncan, so you wanted to look as good as possible, says the little angel sitting on one shoulder.

Because you are in love with her and wanted to make your case, like having your cake and eating it, too, says the little devil sitting on the other one.

I hate them both.

"Levi, until you talk to Buzz, you can't do a thing, so just do what does *not* come natural to you," Mom says. "You've gotta wait."

I tap my head against the back of the chair and stare at the sky. It's hot today, the summer heat is starting to kick in. Maybe I'll take Duncan down to the river for a swim. In case it's my only chance to do it before someone comes along and takes him away from me, that is.

"While you wait, you can do something to figure yourself out, though."

I glance over at my mother, tapping away on her iPad, scrolling through and looking at ice cream recipes. She is obsessed.

I tap my foot on the porch a few times. "What? What can I do to help this?"

"You could dissect the feelings you have for Georgie so you can put that to rest once and for all," she announces matter-of-factly. Austin stands by her chair, nodding his head like a parrot agreeing with its master.

"That's easy for you to say; you don't have skin in the game like I do."

"Skin in the game? You're hiding behind a fictional idea of an engagement. THAT is not having skin in the game, it's playing house or testing the waters. Why buy the cow when you get the milk for free—"

"Pretty sure that's not what that saying means," Austin tries to interject, but Mom won't let him.

"You, no talking." She wags a finger at him. "As his brother, it's your job to make sure he's on the straight and narrow, and this whole plan is not straight nor is it narrow. It is wide and wiggly and has gotten him into trouble."

She then turns to face me again. "However, we're going to fix it."

I raise an eyebrow. "We are?"

She nods. "I feel like you've been attempting to play a long game; you just did it stupidly."

I can't argue. Mother knows best. "Why didn't you, of all people, try to stop me?"

"Because, Levi, something you're going to have to learn if

you do get custody of Duncan is that sometimes you have to let your kids make their own mistakes."

Mic. Drop. MC Mary Porter in the house, ladies and gentlemen.

"Okay, that's fair." I tilt the chair so it teeters on its hind legs. "What do I do now?"

"Put that chair on all four legs before you bust your chin open, that's what," she mumbles, waiting for me to do just that. I do as I'm told because I will never be too old to listen to my mother. Never.

"If you're going to try to woo her," Austin offers while I pray what he's saying is going to actually be helpful, "you also need to talk to her about that social media post I saw."

My mother's lips go into a tight line. "What post?"

Austin opens his phone and shows it to my mother. As soon as she's done, I hold my hand out. I've not seen it yet, only heard about it from Georgie. As I read it over and skim the comments, I can see why she's feeling vulnerable and pulverized by all of this at the moment.

"That poor girl, and you didn't take into account what can of worms could be opened when she's with you." Mom tilts her head to the side as she raises her hand to shield her face from the sun. "Talk about learning a hard lesson."

The brevity of this whole situation sits on my chest like someone dropped a weight on it. The lies being said about my beautiful friend, inside and out, who has been through so much are horrible, and the fact she's been thrust into all of this because I wanted it? I'm feeling like I overstepped here and in a big way.

But is it overstepping when you've been secretly in love with someone for over a year? When their name pops up and you feel a blast of ice go through your veins because you know that they're in the world and under the same sky as you? There were nights when I was on the road and the one thing that kept me going was looking forward to a call with Georgie, glancing up at the moon and knowing she was seeing the same one I was.

"I need to fix things with her, and I need to do it fast." My eyes flicker back and forth between my mother's and Austin's. "But I don't know what to do, and y'all have seen that when I'm left to my own devices, I pick the wrong street to turn down. Help."

"I know!" Austin slaps his hands together. Underneath his tough exterior, this quarterback is also a fan of a Hallmark film or three. "It's time for…" He does a drumroll on his thighs. "The grand gesture!"

My mother cocks her head and looks at him as if he's just suggested we take her to a strip club. "A grand gesture? Like what, buy her a house?"

"I mean, if he had the money…" Austin begins.

Laughing, I cut him off. "Like in a rom-com, Mom. I need to show up and do the big thing to show her how I feel."

"How *do* you feel?" She looks at me pointedly. "Expand on that."

Talk about being open with your family. "I'm in love with her."

The pair fall silent as my words sink in. I'm even stewing on the fact I've said it out loud as my mother starts grinning.

"Well, now that you have FINALLY admitted what we can all see, you really do need to sweep her off her feet." She hops up out of her seat and heads back into the house. "Come on, I'm going to make us something to snack on while we come up with some ideas on how you can woo that sweet girl. I like her and want to keep her around, so let's make it good, hear me?"

"Just no more ice cream," Austin pleads as he follows her inside.

I'm two steps behind them when my cell phone rings.

Glancing at the screen, I see Buzz's name, then hit the button to connect and press it to my ear as fast as I can.

"It's not good news," he says once our niceties are done. "I've had a call from the judge. Turns out she's in Lorna's book club and got an earful earlier today about your situation with your soon-to-be wife." He says the last part with what I can only imagine is a little grimace on his face. I start to remind him that he hinted at this very idea, but instead I decide not to. In the end it was my choice.

"What's happening?" I ask, my stomach starting to knot.

"She managed to get an order to move the date up to next week, Monday morning. I'm sorry for the short notice, Levi, but you'll be going to court after the weekend to see who gets custody of Duncan once and for all."

EIGHTEEN

Georgie

Ever wake up in the life you have and wonder how it got to be such a mess? Yeah, that's how my Saturday is going, too.

I spent all of last night eating my emotions. I couldn't decide if I wanted to power eat cucumber, straight from the Porter's garden, and peanut butter sandwiches (do not knock 'em til you've had them) or eat Mary's lavender ice cream until my stomach burst. I tried to watch something on TV, but gave up and laid on my couch listening to a true crime podcast instead.

There were moments where I forgot that I had spilled the beans to Lorna, setting off a possible avalanche for Duncan and the Porters, and when I was reminded, I would grab my phone, wanting to get lost in social media. Only I couldn't.

Each time I'd open an app, there was that photo of Levi with me. Us. Together. Lips on lips, kisses for days. I mean, not to toot my own horn, but it *is* a great picture. The issue being that I've been tagged again and again in the image, so every time those pictures are shared, I'm notified. It's crazy-making. Intense. Maddening. It's made me never want to go on social media again. Don't even get me started on the comments. The comments section is a whole other sad story that I still can't and don't want to get into. It has sliced me deep.

When I arrived at work this morning, there was another box that had been delivered. I'd opened it hoping it was an order of books, but no. It was a present sent from one of the brands Levi works with.

"Oh my god, this is out of control," I scream-sigh as I kick open the back door of the shop and toss the box inside. It's a chenille throw blanket in a rose color. Not bad really. I can use it to hide under when I walk down the street. It'll have a scarlet letter on it, a C for champagne, since that's what Lorna smelled on my breath. At least it was Veuve Clicquot.

More sighing. I rarely drink, and the one time I do, I have a smackdown with the one person I shouldn't be talking to. It can't get past me, the irony being that I was coming out of a bridal fitting for my fake wedding...oh, it's all quite the full-circle moment, isn't it?

I messed up, but hey, I can say that when I do mess up, I mess up good. I'm still telling myself off as I walk past a mirror in the back room, catching a glimpse of myself in it. My eyes are puffy from crying last night and I want to hug that sad girl I see in the reflection, but also I want to remind her that she's a terrible fake fiancée. I'm sure if I had a ring, now would be the time for Levi to demand it back.

I trot to the front of the store, turn the sign from closed to open and unlock the door, then flip on all of the lights to show that we're ready for business. I don't make it back to the counter before the bell dings behind me, signaling a customer has entered the premises.

I turn around only to find someone who resembles Levi standing in front of me.

"Oh." I gasp, pointing to his eyes and the swelling around his face. "What happened?"

"The cat," he says, pointing to my eyes. "What's your excuse?"

"My stupidity?" I say, shrugging and making him laugh. Just a little.

He looks around the store, his gaze landing back on me. "Can we talk, like outside for a minute?"

"Sure." I reach across the counter and grab my keys. It's a Saturday, so weekend shoppers come in closer to eleven, at least in my experience. I can afford to close the store for a little bit. Seeing as it's for Levi, I really don't mind. "You wanna lead?"

We walk down the street in silence, two Moon Pie-faced residents looking like we got into a fight with a swarm of bees. Spoiler alert: it looks like the bees won. We pass by Mr. Altman, who raises a hand in greeting only to have it float to his mouth in an attempt to cover his shock at the sight of us. I still wave. Me and my puffy-faced man.

At least we have each other. For now, anyway.

Levi beckons down a side path, maneuvering us into a small park off 2nd Street. He sits on a small wrought-iron bench at the back of the park, patting the seat beside him. "Join me?"

I do as he asks, keeping my hands on my knees and looking at the ground. I don't know where to begin, so I wait for him to speak.

The sound of the birds around us pulls me in, their tunes repetitive and familiar, making me feel somewhat at peace. The small park is full of leafy mature trees and quite shady, a great spot to sit as the sun rises to take on the day. You can feel a little heat in the air, but not a lot yet. There's still time in the day for the temperatures to go up.

Beside me, Levi clears his throat. "Things have escalated.

Lorna's managed to get the case moved up on the docket and we're in court on Monday now."

"What?" My mouth hangs open. I'm sick. "It's my fault, Levi. I am so sorry."

"No, you don't get to do that," he says. "This is *my* fault. I should never have asked you to pretend to be anything with me."

I'm not sure what I'm hearing. I think he's saying that he wishes he could take the pretend part of this back, but I'm not sure. Doesn't matter. I want to scream.

"I got carried away. I started screwing around with that stupid registry. It was the temptation of all of those free and amazing things." I sit back against the bench and set my mouth in a straight line. "I got way into it. I picked out all kinds of presents for our fake guests to get us when they come to our fake wedding. And I was so close to picking out our invitations..."

Levi spins to face me. "You what now?"

"Not really," I say, half-laughing, half not. "Well, the part about the invitations, that's a joke. I joke when I'm feeling uncomfortable. The part about the registry is the truth. But hey, there's a bright side."

"What's that?"

"We don't need to be engaged anymore." The reality of what that means hits me, and I have to admit, my heart feels like it just got sucker punched. "You don't *need* me now."

"But that's the thing, Georgie. I do." Levi angles his body so he can take my hands in his. "I used a fake engagement as an excuse to get closer to you. In truth, I've been falling in love with you since day one and I kind of manipulated the situation to my advantage."

Now, that was a mouthful I wasn't ready for.

A tiny smile begins to tug at the corners of my lips. It's like there's an invisible string attached to the ends of my mouth and it's pulling them up, up, up like balloons rising to the sky.

Did Levi Porter just admit he's in love with me?

"You're falling for me?" I spit the words out like a bad taste, but I don't mean to. I'm in shock. Good shock, like the kind I know I'll be resuscitated from, but shock nonetheless.

Levi's look is serious, though. "I am, but I need to know that you're in this with me."

"In this?" I query.

"This. Whatever this next chapter is." He wraps an arm around my shoulders and pulls me against him, using his other hand to push a few strands of hair away from my face as he kisses the tip of my nose. "I want you to be around for all of it."

I. Am. Done.

I nod my head, the tip of my nose rubbing against his as I kiss his lips once, twice, three times for good measure. Or maybe it's for luck. Either way, I got to kiss him three times in a row.

"I do, too," I whisper, keeping my lips hovering over his as he slants his mouth across mine and pulls me in. This kiss isn't like the others we've had. They were good kisses. First kisses, the kind you start with as you're figuring each other out. This kiss? It's the kind of kiss that says there's more going on here. There's cupcakes, rainbows, and a confetti parade with this kiss. It's a kiss that tells my heart it's fine to kick back and enjoy the ride now.

It's also the kiss that says, "Stick around kid, there's more to come." And I'm here for it. It's the kiss throwing hints that this isn't temporary. It's for real. For more than just now, it's forever.

We slow down, with me pulling away first so I can catch my breath. His fingertips dance up and down my spine as he caresses my back. I could stay like this forever if he asked me to.

"So, about this registry," he starts, and I close my eyes. No, I shut them tight. "Did we get anything good, or do we have to take it all back?"

"Well, Adidas sent us an unsolicited chenille throw this morning. Someone knew to send it to the bookstore, which is a phenomenon I'll never figure out." Chuckling, I lean against him, letting my head rest on his shoulder. "There's also this giant metal ostrich that I'm becoming fond of, but I've already spoken to Mr. Altman. Everything will go back to the store this weekend. I may have lied and told him Bex did it as a joke."

Levi throws his head back and laughs, pulling me in close to his chest and holding me tight. "You honestly make me laugh like no one has before. I cannot believe you managed to actually register for our wedding..."

"Well, I'm calling it off now," I say, giggling as I stand. I hold my hand out for him. "I do need to get back to the store to open it for the day, though. Walk me back?"

Levi's eyes rock to my hand before he takes it, his fingers threading through mine. We walk in silence, two people who are both going down their own paths in life and somehow, some way managed to find a spot where these paths cross.

"Do you want me to go with you Monday?" I ask. "To court?"

He nods. "I'm nervous."

Squeezing his hand, I try to jolt him back to the present. "Don't be. You're good for Duncan."

I don't have to be facing him to know that those dark blue eyes of his are swirling with worry. His silence tells me all I need to know. As we make our way back down 2nd Street and turn back onto Magnolia Lane, all I can think is that I want to help. I want to help fix the blunder that has opened up this whole Pandora's Box.

But the only thing I can think of to do could also be the one thing that could break this whole situation. It could actually cause more chaos and anger, if it's not done correctly.

The more I think about it, the more I see a light. A path to fixing this in a more organic way. But it's a risk. I could lose everything, including Levi, if it doesn't go as planned.

It kind of begs the question: How much is all of this worth to me?

NINETEEN

Levi

Pulling up outside of the apartment building where Georgie's staying, I navigate my car into a parking spot. I'd just finished my morning coffee and was still reveling in the fact that the swelling had gone down in my face when Georgie texted me. A pipe had burst this morning and the first floor was flooded.

As soon as I put the SUV in park, I hop out of the vehicle and race up the steps to the front door. I knock on it a few times and wait. I'm a little surprised, to be honest, that she's not out here waiting for me. Her text made it sound like she was on the Titanic and it would go down if I didn't get here in time.

I raise my hand and knock on the door a few more times, wondering where she could be. Backing down the steps, I decide to go around to the back entrance. I spin around only to run straight into Lorna.

"Whoa!" she cries out, putting her hands up to stop me from barreling into her. "Where are you headed so fast?"

What are the odds I would continue to run into this woman all over town? Sweetkiss Creek is small, but come on.

I incline my head toward the building. "Georgie's using my apartment and she said a pipe burst." I move past Lorna and start to walk away only to have her call out behind me.

"Well, I guess I'll wait here for you?"

"Wait for me?" I stop in my tracks, then spin around to face her. "Why?"

She cocks her head to the side and looks at me like I just sprouted ten heads. "Because of that email you had Georgie send me?"

The plot thickens. "What email?"

"The one asking me to meet you here to talk," she huffs.

I'm starting to get an idea here that one bookshop owner may have tried to do the ole switcheroo.

Something out of the corner of my eye catches my attention in the window of the first floor. I look over to find Georgie standing just beyond, peeking around the curtain. She jumps back, trying to disappear into the shadows, but it's too late.

"Georgie," I command with as much authority as I can muster. "Can you open the window for a moment please and clear something up?"

The window slides up and she sticks her head out. "Okay, I know I may have overstepped by lying to you both, but you two need to talk."

"Indeed, young lady, you overstepped," Lorna says, going to her usual stance of hands on hips. "I've got better things to do than be here trying to talk sense into Levi."

"No one needs to talk sense into anyone," I say, feeling slighted. "Anyway, if someone is going to talk sense into anyone, it will be me when I talk to you. I cannot seem to get it through your head that your son wanted me to be..."

"And this is why I tricked you two," Georgie shouts as she claps her hands with each word. She's like a mini Judge Judy. We'll call her Judge Georgie. "Levi, you want the best for that sweet boy and you need to get that across to Lorna without insulting her or reminding her of what her son wanted."

Putting aside the fact I feel like she's just slapped me upside the head, she's right. However, she's not done. She turns to Lorna.

"And you're so busy wanting to win some contest that involves your grandson as the prize, you need to see what is actually going to be good for him. And that's Levi." She then fans her hand in front of us, like a blackjack dealer showing her hand. "Now, I've got my own mess to clean up that doesn't involve a burst pipe, Levi, so stand down. I'll leave this with you two to discuss from here. Good luck, and may you each be able to see the other person's side."

With that, she disappears from our sight and shuts the widow, pulling the curtains tight. I need to hand it to her. She's a low-key genius. Trickster, but genius.

Lorna turns her back to me. "I've got nothing to say that I can't say tomorrow in court."

"Come on, Lorna, let's try talking to each other and see where we get to." I walk around so I'm standing in front of her. "I'll start. I'm sorry."

She glares my way. "For what, exactly?"

"I'm sorry that Tom's gone. I think about him every day and what he would do or want. I think about his marriage to Katie and how lucky I was that I got to be his best man for their nuptials. I think about my first pro game and looking up in the stands and seeing them there, cheering me on." I laugh, the memories of years gone by starting to wind me down. "I'm also sorry for that time you had to get us out of jail because we were egging people's mailboxes in high school."

A tiny snicker escapes her lips. "You two were funny when you were together."

"Your son made me a better man, you know. He was the one who, when we had to do community service for that egging, made me go. I was going to skip it and he would show up at my house to drive me to our check-in." Tom was always the guy who everyone wanted to hang out with, including me. The cool guy who got the best grades, always dated the best girls, and seemed to excel at anything and everything he wanted to do. Like Midas but only he was in high school, and living in Sweetkiss Creek.

"You lived at our house that one summer, when you two did football camp." Some of the anger that had been flashing on her features seems to fade as we chat. "I'll never forget that. Your mom and I spent a lot of time together those days watching you boys play from the stands."

I nod, the memory is fresh for me, too. "I hate that we're here now."

"Me, too." She sighs. "I don't recognize myself right now, Levi. Honestly."

I can see tears welling in her eyes and I know she's in the same place I'm in, where Duncan is but even more so. She's a mother mourning the loss of her only son. Her shoulders shake mildly; I know she's trying to hold back her tears and I feel like an intruder. Even though we're here talking, I feel like this is a very private moment she needs to have and I'm not supposed to be here.

"I keep telling myself that if I have Duncan with me, I can make it all go away. This feeling inside, the one that is eating me up." A tear drops onto her cheek, making its way down the side of her face slowly. "You know, I fought with him the day they died. For a long time, I couldn't remember the last time I told him I loved him."

Her words hit me in the stomach, but they also open my eyes to who she is and why. The pain she's in—it's a mother's pain and filled with intense heat and sadness. All I've done is buck against her, not see her side. I've been fighting her since she laid down the first smack and not putting myself in her shoes. My mother always taught us to look at things from others' perspectives so we can get a better view of the world. Now that I am, I can see she's hurting with more intensity than I ever could have imagined.

"He knows you loved him," I say, and she nods, wiping at her tears.

"I know that now, but it took a while for me to get there." She crosses her arms in front of her chest, as if she's giving herself a hug as she sizes me up. "Goodness, how he loved you. How much they both must have loved you to want you to care for their son. And what does that say about me? That they wouldn't want me to be the one to take over?"

I want to hug this poor woman right now. Everything in me says not to, but instead I decide to just do it. The world needs more hugs anyway, right?

"It doesn't say anything bad about you, Lorna," I say, pulling her into my arms as she collapses against my chest and sobs. We stay like this, unmoving, and I let my own tears start to fall as well.

After a few minutes, she pulls away, wiping at her cheeks as she takes a big breath of air.

"I'm sorry for that, Levi," she says as she smooths back her hair and straightens her shirt. "I don't think I've taken the time to properly mourn them and say goodbye. I've spent too much time focusing on Duncan and keeping him going. I didn't want to fall down on the job, you know?"

"I get it," I say, acknowledging her feelings. "I'm the same. In fact, I've got Duncan in therapy now so he can work on his feelings around their death and I'm going to work on mine, too."

"That's smart." Lorna looks off in the distance. "When you suggested he go to therapy last year, I should have listened. I thought I could make it all better." She waits a beat before looking at me. "I'm starting to see why Tom wanted it to be you," she says sheepishly.

"I want what is best for Duncan. That's you, me, my mom, and Austin." Movement at the front window catches my eye, and I look up to see Georgie has changed locations and is at this window now watching us. "Even that nutbar, Georgie, who I am falling in love with. She is really good for him."

Lorna smiles. It's faint, but it's there. "Really?"

I shove my hands in my front pockets. "He talks to her, you know."

Lorna raises one of her nineties-era thin eyebrows, arching it in surprise. "How did she get him to open up?"

"It's what she does. He likes being around her. He's talking to all of us more these days, and I have to give her the credit." I put my hand on her shoulder. "I want us to be a family, all of us, together if we can. But it's up to the courts now, I guess."

She nods, her eyes rocking up to where Georgie stands before coming back to mine. She reaches up, pats my hand, and then moves it off her shoulder as she steps away.

"I should get going, Levi." She starts to walk off, turning back and pausing for a moment to smile and wave at Georgie. She then looks back my way. "She is special, that one. That took some straight-up gumption to invite both of us here like she did today. This could have gone a lot worse."

With a final bow of her head, she turns around and walks away.

Leaving me with a little more insight into a woman who is hurting way more deeply than I'd known she was before.

TWENTY

Georgie

The early morning sunlight streams into the first-floor apartment, casting a warm golden glow across the room. I'd woken up early, expecting the arrival of the Porter family. They'd decided over the weekend it would be best for them to use Levi's Sweetkiss Creek apartment as their meeting place, or green room, before heading to the courthouse.

Once I manage to get Toto out of his bed and into the backyard, I pour myself a cup of coffee before heading to the living room to sit, sip, and wake up. The light dances through the sheer curtains I hung the other day, painting delicate patterns on the walls and floor. Every corner is illuminated by the morning sunlight, turning the space into a tranquil sanctuary. I've come to enjoy staying here over the past week, but based on the phone call I'd gotten yesterday, my days here are done. My landlord had been excited to let me know my place was ready and I could move back in this week, if I wanted to.

Outside, the world is awake and pumping. A small amount of traffic makes its way down the street, and a horn honks just outside, signaling one of the neighbors being picked up for work. The sounds of birds chirping fill the air, mingling with the soft rustle of...my door handle being jiggled back and forth over and over again.

There's a knock at the door. I take a few long strides across the living room to open the door, finding Duncan on the other side of it grinning up at me.

He holds up a paper bag in front of him. "We brought donuts."

"I like donuts," I say, taking the bag from his outstretched hand as he trots past me. Mary marches up the steps, a tight smile stretched across stressed features, with Austin right behind her, both of them sipping coffee in to-go cups.

"Good morning," she says, kissing my cheek as she makes her way past. "Sorry for this early morning intrusion."

"It's a big day," I say as I turn and wait for Levi to lock the doors of his SUV. Swinging a garment bag over his shoulder, he jogs over and takes the steps two at a time to come up to greet me, wrapping his arms around me and pulling me in tight to his chest as he does.

Even in this moment where his and Duncan's future hangs in such delicate balance, I know inside of me with all my heart that I am in love with this man. Forget the falling part, I've already face-planted. I'm his.

His smell has changed; today's cologne makes me think of clean sheets in the wind, hanging outside on a summer after-noon. There's a note of coffee and peppermint, but that comes when he brushes his lips across mine.

"Hey," he whispers, pressing his forehead against mine and closing his eyes. "You sleep okay?"

Nodding, I kiss the tip of his nose. "Thank you for not being mad about yesterday."

He pulls away and treats me to a half-smile. "You were trying to solve the problem. I can't be mad at you for that." He nods toward the house. "I should get Duncan dressed and ready for court."

I follow him as he goes inside, grabbing Duncan as we head to the back bedroom. I'd already showered and dressed, clearing the path in case anyone needed the bathroom. However, when I look closer at Levi and Duncan, they're both already in their suits.

"I thought you were using this place as your staging area today?" I picked up the garment bag. "What's in here?"

Levi unzips it and pulls out their jackets and a couple of matching ties. This small gesture brings a smile to my face, and to Duncan's.

"You got me a tie like yours?" he asks, beaming.

"Of course," Levi responds, putting the tie around Duncan's neck. I watch as he threads the material and loops it through, his hands deftly moving as if they've done this a million times before. The tie, a deep navy blue, contrasts beautifully against Duncan's crisp white shirt, adding a touch of sophistication to his already handsome, and quite grown up, appearance.

Levi adjusts the knot with practiced ease, his fingers brushing against Duncan's collar in a way that's both parental and casual.

"Will you teach me how to do this one day?" Duncan inquires as Levi steps back to admire his handiwork.

Levi shoots me a look, his eyes a bit woeful. "I hope so, buddy."

It only takes him another second before he puts the finishing touches on Duncan's tie and hands him his jacket. Levi looks at his watch. "It's eight o'clock now. We've got a few more minutes before we have to leave and meet Buzz, so if you're going to have a donut, get one now from Austin, okay? But nothing with powdered sugar."

Duncan nods before zipping out the bedroom door,

small little boy feet flying down the hallway at the mere mention of sugar. There's a bittersweet knock at my heart as I turn around to see what Levi's doing and find him standing and facing the bedroom mirror, his own hands shaking, struggling with his own tie mere seconds after taking care of Duncan's.

"Here," I say, stepping in front of him and taking the tie from his hands. The weight of the day and the gravity of what's about to happen must be hitting home for him. This is one thing I can do to help. "Let me. Being in foster home after foster home, you end up having a lot of 'brothers' who need help, always, with their ties."

"So you come with experience." He tries joking, but without a smile or laughter in your voice can it be considered one?

It's my turn to fold the fabric over, looping it around and making the knot tight but not too tight so we can adjust as needed. The hint of coffee and peppermint is back, his breath warm as he stands here and takes deep breaths, trying to calm himself. I wish I could help, and make his pain my own, but I can't.

Stepping back, I admire my work, like Monet or Degas must have done when they'd finish a masterpiece. Only Levi is his own masterpiece, really; I'm just the lucky girl who got to call him my fiancé for a brief, if not insane, moment in time.

As I smooth his tie and help him put on his jacket, there's a knock at the front door.

"Grab it, Austin?" Levi calls out before he looks at me with an odd expression. "You're not expecting anyone right now, are you?"

I shake my head. "At this hour? No way."

We both pause, ears to the door listening to garbled conversation as it floats down the hallway to the back of the place. A moment later, the clicking sound of Mary's heels on the hardwood floor as she makes her way back to where we're lurking breaks our silence.

"Hey," she says, stepping into the bedroom. She has her eyes on me but drags them to Levi. "Someone is at the door for you."

Levi starts to follow her, turning around and grabbing my hand as he does.

"Come with me?" He kisses the back of my hand. "I need you to be by my side for all of this today."

"You got it." I point to the door. "You lead?"

We walk in silence to the front, not sure who could be waiting to see Levi. I can tell you this much, I am not expecting to see Lorna when we walk into the living room, but there she is, standing and clutching the side of the front door. Her face looks as if it's been pulled tight in the same way Mary's does. It's the look of a mother who wants to help her children, but can't.

"Glad you're here." She looks at me, nodding a hello. "Can I talk to you for a minute outside, Levi?"

"Of course," he says as he goes outside, his hand still clutching mine. As we walk down the steps to the sidewalk with Lorna, she turns around and puts her purse on the ground.

"I came to say a few things before this morning unfolds." She's nervous today, I can tell by the way she fidgets with her hands. It's not something I've ever seen her do before.

She looks at me first, taking me by surprise. "Thank you for tricking me yesterday. It's something most people would never do. I've got to say, I didn't think it was a smart move until I left here and was home replaying the meeting, and like I told Levi, it took some guts to do what you did."

"Thanks?" I manage, unsure what to say here.

Lorna chuckles. "I know it's an odd way to show gratitude, but what you did is show me how much you care about

Duncan in that one move. You were willing to risk upsetting Levi by forcing us to talk about Duncan's future and welfare." She then does something I'm for sure not prepared for: she reaches out and takes my hand and smiles at me. With genuine warmth and appreciation. "What you did yesterday was the most motherly move of all, and I wanted you to know that I see you."

I'm stunned. Shocked. Flabbergasted and silenced. I want to cry and hug her because I feel like I know where this might be going, but I'm too scared to move. Instead, I squeeze her hand before she pulls it away and turns her attention to the hulk of a man beside me.

"I'm dropping the case." Sighing, she clasps her hands in front of her while Levi's jaw goes slack.

"You are?" he asks, excitement in his voice.

"I can't do it anymore. Not when it's for all the wrong reasons." Her eyes meet mine. "You helped me see that, Georgie. I've been fighting for something I'll never get back, and I need to deal with that on my own."

No one says a word. I'm afraid to breathe, to even disturb the force at this very moment.

"I would ask you if you're sure, Lorna, but I want this to be over too badly," Levi says, honestly, after a moment. "I guess what I should say is thank you."

She smiles at Levi, taking both of his hands into her own. "No, thank you for dealing with a crazy woman who needs some time to grieve. I do plan on taking you up on the offer to be together as much as we can as a family, though—"

"Are you kidding? Of course!" Levi says, pulling her in for a hug. "I cannot imagine anything better than for Duncan to have the best of everything, and we can give him that."

As he releases Lorna from his embrace, she looks back at me once more. "I know we can. All of us. That is one very lucky young man."

"He is," I say, looking back over my shoulder. I half expect to see a small crowd gathered at the window, but no one's there. Guess they're not as nosy as I would be if it was me.

"Okay, then," Lorna says, picking up her bag and throwing it over her shoulder. "I'm sure Buzz will be calling you soon to let you know you don't have to go to court. I already called my lawyer on the way over here. You should go, celebrate, and ring in your new beginning."

She looks at us, sadness etched on her features as she fights through a smile, turning on her heel to walk away. Levi grasps my hand again, threading his fingers through mine as I look at him, my eyes silently pleading. I'm sending him a message, so I hope he can read my mind.

"Lorna," I called out, letting go of his hand so I could jog a few steps to meet her. "We probably will go celebrate and have breakfast somewhere, but you should join us. Right, Levi?"

When I turn around, Levi's already nodding in agreement. "I most certainly do. I think that we should start a tradition today for a weekly family meal." He wraps an arm around my shoulders as I let those words sink in.

He means it for me, too. Not just for Duncan. Not for Lorna. For us.

Family.

Lorna's eyes bounce back and forth between us before she bursts out into tears, covering her face with her hands. Instinct tells me to give her a moment, so I do. In a few seconds, she puts her hands down and is laughing through her tears.

"Yes! Yes, I'd love to go to breakfast and I'd love to make this a weekly tradition." She digs in her purse, pulling out a wad of tissues to dab at her cheeks.

"Well, follow me, then," Levi says as he steps forward and takes her hand. "Let's go inside and get the others. We'll let Duncan pick the place."

I stay on the street, watching as Levi and Lorna go back up

the steps and inside the apartment. This is a moment I want to sear into my memory banks for always so I can tell Duncan about it one day. How his grandmother and Levi made peace in order to give him the life he deserves.

How they became a family.

"Hey," Levi calls out, gripping the door handle still. "We need you in here."

"Really?" I ask. I make my way up the steps as Duncan appears in the doorway beside him.

"I need you," Duncan says, pointing to his tie, which has already come untangled. "Austin messed my tie up, but Levi says you know how to fix it."

Grinning, I hold my hands out to my side. "Guilty as charged, I'm good at tying ties."

Duncan giggles. "Tying ties. That's going to be the title of the first book I write."

"Is it?" I say, smiling over his head at Levi. "I like that. I can see you being an author."

Levi ruffles his hair, a move I love watching him do. "Okay, buddy, let's get the family together and get some food, okay?"

Duncan nods, his eyes still trained on me. "You heard him. Come on, Georgie, I need to get the family together."

My heart hiccups in a way that I'm not comprehending. As Duncan holds his hand out for me to take, and I do, I'm hit by a wall of emotion and overwhelm.

Family. Even Duncan sees me as family, and it's more than reciprocated. I feel this in my bones as pure and solid as the Earth is round and rotating in a circle, orbiting the sun.

I don't care what else there is to this life. This moment of acceptance is all I've ever needed.

Ever.

TWENTY-ONE

Georgie

"So, if I'm going to be an author, I figured I should start a journal." Duncan hoists a giant five-subject notebook on the counter in front of me. "I'm going to write in it every day and put down what I did."

"That's a good idea," I say casually as I price the stack of books in front of me. "Have you started already?"

"On Sunday, after our first Sunday dinner with Grandma." He pats the notebook and slides it my way. "Can you keep it back there for now? I don't want to lose it while I'm here working my shift."

"Sure." I slide it under the counter. Duncan has been with me at the store almost every day for the last ten days, ever since Lorna called off the court case. It's been blissful and surreal as we've all settled into a new pattern, routines that needed to be there, and now that they are we're all benefiting from them. Even Toto, who is getting walked twice a day by Duncan now as well as serious playtime in the park, usually after work.

"You know, we shouldn't call it a shift since technically you're not supposed to be 'working,'" I tease.

"Well, you're paying me in books, so we can't be breaking the law."

Wise guy. Still witty and I'm still not going to let him know I think so. Don't want it going to his head.

"Good point." I grab the stack of books and head into an aisle, placing them on their designated shelves. "Are you looking forward to moving into your new place with Levi this weekend?"

"Yeah!" Duncan cries out, jumping in place. "We'll be in town now, so that is cool. I can go to the park when I want to, but we'll still go to the farm, too. That's also cool."

"Everything is cool." I giggle.

"You bet it is," Duncan says excitedly. "Maybe Toto can even come stay with us sometimes?"

"Maybe," I say with a shrug. "Toto is kind of happy in his old place now, though."

Even if our old place has had a semi-makeover. With the help of Levi, Austin, and Duncan, I'd moved my boxes back into my apartment over the weekend, having renewed my lease for one more year. Only Levi managed to pull a fast one on me and surprise me. He'd told me that he and Austin would go out to my storage unit, get my furniture, and meet me at my place to move it back in.

When I arrived at my apartment, ready to move furniture, Levi stood on the porch holding his hands up in the air as if he was surrendering. "Do not be mad at me."

He led me inside, and when he opened the door to my place, I discovered it was fully furnished with all new things. I'd navigated my way from room to room, my jaw dragging on the ground. He'd gone to Altman's and repurchased a lot of the items I had on our fake bridal registry and outfitted my home totally under the radar.

"Levi said you got a signing bonus for your contract negotiations," Duncan says as he joins me in front of the shelves. "What kind of contract did you negotiate?"

"I'll explain it to you one day," I respond, reaching out and ruffling his hair in much the same way Levi does. This kid still needs a haircut, and I'm going to make him an appointment today.

The ding of the bell over the front door signals a new customer. I stand up and head to the front, surprised to find a florist there with the largest bouquet of flowers I've ever seen.

"Are you Georgie Simpson?" the delivery man asks as I nod. "Sign here."

I sign the sheet of paper he presents to me on a clipboard, watching as he places the bouquet on the front counter by the cash register. It's so large that there's no more room on the counter, not even if anyone wanted to buy a book.

"You're sure it's for me?"

The guy rolls his eyes and leaves, the bell ringing as he lets himself out.

"They're pretty!" Duncan exclaims as we walk over to inspect the arrangement together. Lilies, roses, hyacinths, and more are stuffed into a beautiful glass vase. All of my favorites blended into one beautiful bundle.

I snatch the card that came with it from its hiding spot amongst the greenery, tearing open the envelope to see who sent them. When I slide the card out, I'm surprised to find there's nothing on it. Just an "X."

"Who's it from?" Duncan asks, so I show him the card.

"Huh." That's all he says. It's one word, but it's weighted. I've got this kid's number, you know.

"What does that 'huh' mean?" I say, narrowing my eyes as he giggles.

"Nothing, but maybe you'll see," he sings, clapping his hands together as the bell rings and the door opens again behind me.

Spinning around, I'm really surprised to see Mr. Altman hefting the giant metal ostrich I'd just returned back inside the store.

Mr. Altman in the bookstore with an ostrich? It's like playing Clue.

"What is that for?" I ask incredulously as he places it beside the counter. "I don't need that now."

"It's for you," he says with a smirk, shooting a wink in Duncan's direction. Beside me, Duncan claps in delight.

As Mr. Altman scoots out of the store, I turn around and place a hand on my hip. First eyeing the flowers, then the ostrich, then Duncan.

"Why do I feel like you know more than you're letting on?"

"Because I do," he squeals.

Note to Future Georgie: this kid will be terrible at surprises. Tell him nothing.

Laughing, I stare at him, wanting to shake him down for more info. "Duncan, you need to tell me what's going on."

Instead of responding, he just points outside to the street behind me. "Look out there."

I turn around slowly, finding Levi standing on the sidewalk holding a giant sign. The words "I LOVE YOU" are clear as day, but it's also been decorated, quite possibly by a very creative ten-year-old, with little scribbles all over it.

As I open the door to walk outside, Duncan yells out, "It's a grand gesture!"

Fighting his own laughter, Levi waves the sign in the air for a couple of seconds before he drops it to his side. "Well, did it work?"

"Your grand gesture?" I say, reaching out to take the sign and look at it closer. It's not just scribbling on the giant piece of cardboard, it's a story of the last few weeks. There's a drawing of a cup with what looks like lemons next to it, signifying my lemonades, ice cream cones, what must be Toto but kinda looks like a dark black lump with ears. But that's okay, I'm sure he'd be happy to be included and not offended.

There's also a farm, a stack of books, and a bookstore sign —Pages and Prose to be precise—and there's a picture of a man and woman, stick figures of course, holding hands with a little boy, while nearby another man and woman are floating above them.

I point to the stick people, grinning. "I guess this is us, and your mom and Austin?"

"Yes and no," Levi says, pointing to the stick drawing of the man, woman, and child. "This one is us with Duncan." He then slides his finger to the other man and woman, floating above and shows me something I didn't see before.

"These are wings. Angel wings, as Duncan said." Levi's blue eyes slam into mine. "It's Tom and Katie watching us."

My hand flies to my heart. I've been sucker punched by a ten-year-old kid.

"This is more than a grand gesture, it's a declaration." Levi reaches out and takes my hand. "I love you."

"I know," I say, threading my arms around his neck. "I love you, too. I think I always have."

"Over the last few weeks, I've thought a lot about us. How we've been slowly getting to know each other over the last year or so, and how for me it's always been you. I can't imagine it not being you by my side as I move into a whole new phase of my life."

"A new phase?" I tilt my head to one side.

"I signed a letter of resignation for my team this morning. I'll do one more season, but next year is my last. The press release will come out tomorrow." His gaze is pulled over my shoulder, and I turn to see Duncan in the doorway inspecting the ostrich. Levi then drags his eyes slowly back to mine.

"Things have changed. I want something different now and it's here in Sweetkiss Creek, not on the road."

I'm pretty sure if one was to describe the look on my face they'd call it flabber-confused. It's beyond surprise. "Are you serious?"

"It's what I want." Levi then raises his hand in the air, snapping his fingers. In a flash, Duncan is by his side, handing him a small box. I watch in stunned silence as Levi drops to one knee, opening the box to present the most beautiful emerald and diamond ring I have ever seen.

"One thing we didn't do right when we got—" He clears his throat, putting his hand to his mouth as he speaks out the side of it. "Engaged," he whispers. "We never got you a ring."

He takes the tiny bauble from its box, holding it in the air for me to see.

"Georgina Simpson, I cannot and will not spend another day without you by my side."

"Me neither," Duncan adds for good measure, making both of us crack up.

"And because of that, I need to ask you if you will please do me..." He then wraps an arm around Duncan. "Do us the honor of becoming my wife?"

The world around me stops. It's quiet. I don't hear the cars driving by, the sound of a resident arguing with the meter maid. I'm pretty sure a dog was barking, but nope. Can't hear that either. I can't make out anything except for my heart beating so loud it sounds as if it is inside my head.

That and I scream "YES!"

Throwing myself into Levi's waiting arms, I kiss him, but only the G-rated version because...well, we've got a young, impressionable boy standing with us, jumping up and down.

With Levi's arms around me, I throw my head back and laugh.

I love this life. I love this man. I love this kid.
I love this.
It's my forever. I've finally found my own forever home.
My version of family and it is amazing.

"Can I see it again?" Bex asks, but I feel like the words were mostly a warning because she grabs my hand before I answer and grins. "I mean, this thing is HUGE! I can see my reflection in it."

A cheer erupts, reverberating in the room around us and in the stadium outside the window where we sit. It's the National Football Conference Championship and the highlight of the day this year; it's Porter versus Porter in the last showdown before the Super Bowl and they're playing in Charlotte. The winning team today goes on to the Super Bowl.

Beside me, Duncan taps my arm. "Can I get more food now?"

The family VIP box at the football games has become this boy's playground. When Levi made the decision to retire at the end of this year, we'd sat down and mapped out a plan for us. He managed intermittent trips, coming home to Sweetkiss Creek as often as he could so he could be present for Duncan, and, ahem, for me since we have a wedding to plan, and in return Duncan and I did everything we could to get to his games every weekend so we could support him.

There were homework meltdowns in airports and a series of Monday mornings skipped at school, but watching Duncan's eyes light up as he watched Levi play and got to travel the United States with us has been the best reward ever.

I check over my shoulder, making sure there's still food for this little scavenger to dig into and he's in luck. One of the room attendants was busy refilling the luncheon platter with fresh sandwiches.

"Of course, but," I wag a finger in the air, "you have to eat all of your dinner tonight. Promise?"

I hold out my pinky, and he wraps his in mine. "Pinky swear," he whispers before racing off to fill his belly.

"You guys are so good with him," Bex says, her voice low as he walks off. "He's grown so much over the last, what, six or seven months?"

I smile at the thought of my first meeting with Duncan. His appearance as a tiny thief in the back of my bookstore is almost erased from my memory. "It's all Duncan. Levi, too. He wants to see Duncan thrive, so he's worked hard. Therapy, bonding sessions..."

My voice trails off as I look across the room at Lorna, who sits in a chair beside Mary, both women laughing and cheering together.

"And Lorna, huh?" Bex puts an arm around my shoulders and gives me a giant squeeze, the way only your bestest girlfriends can. Because she knows the subtext of the entire story from being here on the sidelines through the whole thing. "That relationship has done the biggest one-eighty."

Lorna's eyes meet mine across the room and she waves, her smile big and happy as Duncan jogs over to sit with her and Mary as he noshes on a sandwich.

"Yeah," I say with a grin I can't hide, curling my lips upward. "I feel personally responsible for that one."

Bex grabs my arm and we throw ourselves back into our

seats, cackling, as another cheer breaks the air. Around us, everyone in the room is up on their feet and screaming. Not to be outdone, but also confused because I wasn't paying attention, we both shot up and pressed our faces back to the window, scanning the field. As I do, I realize what the extra loud cheering is all about.

"Look," tapping on the window, I show Bex, "Austin is covering Levi and about to tackle him!"

We watch the two giant Porter boys clash together on the field, Austin taking his brother down and stopping the play.

Bex gasps, grabbing my arm. "Is that legal, can a tight end cover a wide receiver?"

My head spins as I look at Bex. "Wow, you've gotten the lingo down."

"Well," she says with a blush, "I like knowing things. I've taken the time to learn football since I've gotten to know you. Before, I never got it. It was a long stupid game, but had good snacks."

Giggling, we sit back down as someone calls a time-out and Bex waves her hand at the field. "And that's another reason why it's not my favorite. Too many stops. I tell you, if you want to watch a game where there's some insane strength and power, rugby is a great sport."

"Well, Levi's not allowed to play that, there's no helmets. I need him around." Settling back into my seat, I sip my drink and scan the room. This time my eyes land on the tiny Barbie-doll blonde in the back corner, Austin's current influencer girlfriend, who is busy taking selfies and posting to social media.

I've been around Stacey a few times now, and she's easily the most selfish woman I've come across in ages. Look, I'm always going to support other women, and since the incident with Duncan, I've learned not to judge a book by its cover (pun not intended), but sometimes a vapid thing is just a vapid thing.

I've witnessed her giving her number to other football players and flirting with the owners on more than one occasion. I'm pretty sure her intentions aren't the greatest, but Levi's put me in a cone of silence for the time being.

My face gives my inner thoughts away. "What's the look for, puss face? It's like you sucked a lemon."

"Oh, just Stacey." I pull my eyes off the girl, focusing back on the game. "I don't like how she treats Austin."

"Have you said anything?"

"Not allowed. Levi thinks we shouldn't interfere with his brother's love life. He's tried to protect him in the past, but he's gotten defensive. Even stopped talking to Levi for six months once when he was dating someone that Levi didn't get along with." Shaking my head, I cast a sideways glance at Bex. "With those boys, I've learned to let them figure it out."

"They're blood. I get it." Bex shakes her head, eyes scanning the field and landing on Austin's side. "Do you think he'll come to his senses?"

Now, this sentence piques my interest. "I guess, I mean, I hope so. Why are you asking?"

Bex shrugs. "Dunno. I've gotten to know him more and I just want to see the best for him."

"Huh." Narrowing my eyes, I cross my arms in front of me. "Do you have a crush?"

"What?" she almost shrieks. "No. No way! I've seen that man date all kinds of women in the short time I've got to know him. He's a friend, but I wouldn't set him up with one of my friends, and I for sure would not date him. He gets around."

"Okay, just checking in. Not that I would mind if you had one," I say with a chuckle, my eyes landing on Stacey again.

"At least you watch the game and don't post selfies the whole time."

"No, not yet," she teases, waving her hands in the air. "Anyway, we should talk about something more fun, like your upcoming wedding. I love a spring wedding!"

Grinning, I glance at my engagement ring as I settle back into the plush seat of the VIP box, the excitement in the air palpable and snapping with electricity as the game picks up speed right in front of us with the timer beginning to count-down. The stadium buzzes with energy, the crowd roaring with every play.

From my vantage point, the field is spread out in front of us, almost like a vibrant tapestry. The players may be mere specks in the distance, but I can make out Levi's position. Pride wells inside of me for him. His team is down in points and probably won't win this game, but that's fine. He's my forever MVP.

I follow the ball's trajectory, watching the madness unfold, my heart racing with each pass and tackle. Then, a sudden hush falls over the crowd as a clash between the teams forces a pile-up. A whistle blows, players untangling themselves, step-ping away with arms waving in the air. There's an intensity to their actions that signals something more foreboding.

A player is down.

My heart leaps to my throat as I stand, clawing at the glass, my eyes meeting Mary's across the room as we both try to hide our worry.

Snapping my focus back to the field, I look for Levi's number among the throng of people and finally, I'm rewarded when I see him. Only he's rushing and pushing himself through the small crowd gathered around the man down.

"Oh, my..." Bex grabs my hand, her hand flying to her mouth as a chill whips across my body. "It's Austin. He's injured."

Time seems to slow as medics rush onto the field. Panic grips me as I watch them attend to Austin, my mind swirling with fear and worry. In a moment, Mary's hand is on my other arm.

"Come with me, please?" She looks over at Lorna, who sits with Duncan. The two women have a silent exchange that's all-knowing. Motherly. "They'll wait here. I don't feel good about this and want to be in the locker room when they bring him off the field."

I don't say a word. I take Mary's hand and lead her toward the exit, stopping by Stacey's seat as I do. The kicker is that I have to get her attention, she's busy posting a TikTok. My eyes want to roll to the back of my head, and I fight the urge to take the phone from her hands and throw it onto the field.

"Austin's injured. Are you coming?" I should try to engage more, but I don't have the energy.

Stacey looks around the room, peeking out onto the field for a moment before turning her attention back to me. "Ummm, is it cool if I stay here? Maybe text me and I'll meet you guys when you know how he's doing?"

Mary's grip on my hand tightens as my jaw goes slack. I'm frozen with a touch of anger gluing me to my spot, but thankfully, Bex is here.

"Come on," she says, opening the door that leads out to the hall. "I'll walk you guys down and see if I can help get you any news."

Turning away from the now silent room, which was full of excitement and enthusiasm mere moments ago, the three of us headed downstairs to the belly of the stadium.

Bex

Today was supposed to be a day of celebration; either one Porter or the other was walking off this field a champion. The media had a field day in the run up to the game with Porter versus Porter headlines, but they made it this far. That, in itself, is incredible. They're *both* champions. On the field and off, but that's just my opinion.

The hallway outside the Thunderbolts locker room is charged with anxiety. I hurry ahead of Georgie and Mary, hoping to find someone, anyone, from Austin's team who can tell us what's going on. All the while, my head is still trying its best to wrap itself around the fact that his girlfriend couldn't even be bothered to come with us.

I've seen it before. The hanger-oners are what we called them when I was in Los Angeles. Working in the entertainment industry, you get all types of people. Hanger-oners are the people who like to be close to the people who get *the* attention, the stars of the show. Only in this case, it's the football player. Thanks to Taylor Swift and Travis Kelce for making it even cooler to date a guy in the NFL, but like adopting a pet, it's something you have to think about. There's a lot that comes with it...sadly, more times than not, these attention bunnies, as I like to call them, are in it for the wrong reasons.

An official-looking man wearing a team jacket jogs past me. When I see him stop at the locker room door, I make a move.

"Excuse me," I call out, pointing to the door. "I'm with Austin Porter's family. Is he inside? Can we see him?"

The older man stares at me, his face etched with worry as he shakes his head. "I'm sorry, but I can't even take his family to him right now. He's about to be transported by ambulance to the hospital."

A blast of ice water courses through me. "Can I ask what's going on?"

Behind me, the sound of footsteps slowing to a stop alerts

me that Mary and Georgie have caught up to me. The man's focus rocks to each of us as he takes a big breath, looking at Mary.

"Mrs. Porter," the man murmurs, recognizing Austin's mother. "Austin's injured his knee. We're not sure how bad it is, but he can't stand on his own."

Mary's hand flies to her mouth as Georgie holds her. I'm fighting a swell of emotions, ones I'm certainly not expecting to surface right now and they're ones I don't have time to deal with. I do not have any time to unpack feelings that may or may not be rising to the surface for Austin.

"We need to check for a concussion, he was hit with intense force. He'll be going to the local hospital soon." He steps forward to squeeze her arm. "I'm sorry, that's all I know and can tell you right now, but I will let them know you're on the way."

With a heavy sigh, he turns on his heel, opens the locker room door, and disappears. Leaving the three of us standing here in the hallway. We may be surrounded by people milling about, but there's a feeling of being oh-so-very alone. Surreal. Stunned.

Austin. The fear he must be going through, the pain he could be in. My heart pounds in my chest for him. And Stacey. Useless. Sitting upstairs, on her butt, posting photos or stories or TikToks...I do not care. She's heartless, asking us to text her when we know something. Like she deserves to know.

I look at Mary, who is all but crumbling in front of me.

"Come ladies," I say, pulling my car keys out of my pocket. "We know what hospital he's going to and we'll be there when he arrives. Yeah?"

Mary nods silently, tears starting to slowly trickle down her cheeks. Catching Georgie's eyes, she mouths the words 'thank you' to me. I don't need her to do that, this is just what you do. You take care of each other when the going gets tough...you don't post a selfie.

"It's settled. Follow me."

There is strength in numbers, there's the power of three. Like on that TV show Charmed. Three women, three strong women, backing each other up.

Our small gang makes its way to the parking lot exit, arms wrapped around each other and unsure what to expect once we get to where we're going, but it's fine.

Because we have each other.

***

Thank you for reading *The Art of Falling in Love with Your Fake Fiancé!* If you want to read a special BONUS epilogue and attend Georgie and Levi's wedding (and find out more about Austin's health), you can click here to download it now.
*

Bex and Austin's story is coming soon, *The Art of Falling in Love with Your Grumpy Neighbor.* Preorder now if you'd like it to be delivered to your eReader on release in **August '24.**

**If you're reading this book in paperback, you can go to my website www.annekemp.com and sign up for my newsletter. With that, you will get access to the Bonus Epilogue so you don't miss out!*

Thank you!

VIP Acknowledgments

I have some rockstars who support me in the times when I REALLY need it, and two of them are **Andrea Payne** and **Tara Higgins!**

Theses two are on my Beta Team *and* both have helped contribute to the Sweetkiss Creek Series in different ways! For their help and constant support (and hour!) I am always thankful.

THANK YOU to the both of you for being amazing. I'm so glad we connected!!

If you've downloaded and read the Bonus epilogue (you can find it here) you'll be briefly introduced to a couple of new faces, **Kaci** and **Lissa.** These two besties are the best hype squad a girl could ask for.

THANK YOU BOTH for your constant encouragement, kind words, and for always knowing how and when to make me laugh! So happy to have you a part of this world.

Acknowledgments

To my ARC team: THANK YOU for reading, reviewing, and for giving me your thoughts and feedback. YOU ARE THE BEST OUT THERE!!

To my dogs who I ignored while writing this book...we'll go for a very long walk now. Even to the beach. Whatever you want, guys :)

To my husband Glen: thank you for being interested in what I do and always asking questions. I love you!

To you, the person reading this...Thank you for reading this far and for being on this journey with us. I'm not kidding when I say it takes a village to do the things. Your support makes my heart blow up with love. **THANK YOU!!**

About the Author

Anne Kemp is an author of romantic comedies,
sweet contemporary romance, and chick lit.
She loves reading (and does it ridiculously fast, too!), gluten-
free baking
(because everyone needs a hobby that makes them crazy), and
finding time to binge-watch her favorite shows. She grew up in
Maryland but made Los Angeles her home until she
encountered her own real-life meet-cute at a friend's wedding
where she ended up married to one of the groomsmen.
For real.

Anne now lives on the Kapiti Coast in New Zealand, and even
though she was married at Mt. Doom, no...she doesn't have a
Hobbit. However, she and her husband do have a terrier
named George Clooney and a rescue pup named Charlie.
When she's not writing, she's usually with them taking a long
walk on the river by their home.

Sweetkiss Creek Series

Welcome to Sweetkiss Creek, where the locals are nosy, the dogs are pushy, and love could be just around the corner...

The Sweetkiss Creek series are closed door rom coms, filled with close friendships, swoony kisses, and lots of laughs!

The Art of Falling in Love with Your Best Friend

Dylan and Reid's story

friends-to-lovers

The Art of Falling in Love with Your Enemy

Etta and Zac's story

enemies to lovers + grumpy sunshine

The Art of Falling in Love with the Movie Star

Amelia and Spencer's Christmas story

second chance celebrity romance

The Art of Falling in Love with Your Brother's Best Friend

Riley and Jake's story

enemies to lovers + ice hockey star

The Art of Falling in Love with Your Fake Fiancé

Georgie and Levi's story

Thank you for reading!

The Art of Falling in Love with Your Grumpy Neighbor

Bex and Austin's story

Coming August '24!

Love in Lake Lorelei Series

Ahhh...Lake Lorelei, the small town down the road from Sweetkiss Creek. These sweet romcoms are sizzling with chemistry and bringing you all the feels.

Get to know this small town, its locals and, most importantly, the Lake Lorelei Fire Department!

Sweet Summer Nights (Book 1)

Freya and Wyatt's story

The Sweet Spot (Book 2)

Ari and Carter's story

When Sparks Fly (Book 3)

Maisey and Jack's story

The Abby George Series

The Abby George books are closed-door, Chick lit comedies with a lil' sass, a touch of sarcasm, and some innuendo, but guaranteed to have you laughing out loud as you fall in love!

Rum Punch Regrets

Gotta Go To Come Back

Sugar City Secrets

Caribbean Romance Novella

Part of the Abby George world but can be read as a stand alone story.

This book is a sweet and clean closed door romantic comedy.

Second Chance for Christmas

Stay up-to-date on new releases, get special bonus content, and special promotions when you sign up for

Anne's newsletter.

If you're reading this book in paperback, you can go to my website www.annekemp.com and sign up for my newsletter so you don't miss out!